THE KINGDOM OF DOG

NEIL S. PLAKCY

A GOLDEN RETRIEVER MYSTERY

This book is for Jacoplax's Samwise Gamgee, the best golden retriever in the world, and for his daddy.

A big sloppy golden thank you to Miriam Auerbach, Mike Jastrzebski, Christine Kling and Sharon Potts, for their help in bringing this book together, and to Nancy Ann Gazo, my beta reader. Sam appreciates the great care he gets at the Hollywood Animal Hospital from Dr. Jim Herrington and the rest of the staff, and all those who have a hand in preparing his treats, his dinners and his rawhide chew toys.

Behavior Modification

Rochester nudged my knee as I was trying to write a press release. "What's the matter, boy? You need to go out?"

I looked down at the golden retriever by my side. But instead of jumping up, he flopped down and rolled on his back, wagging his paws in the air like a stranded beetle.

"I don't have time to play. I have work to do. Somebody has to pay for your kibbles and bits."

That was the wrong thing to say. Rochester immediately hopped up and looked at me with big brown eyes. "Fine. One treat. Then you go lay down."

He shook his head again, but I handed him the treat anyway. I kept a vacuum-sealed jar on my office desk, filled with tiny treats in the shape of T-bone steaks. He gobbled the tidbit, then trotted across the room, where he sprawled in front of the French doors and rested his head on his paws, staring at me.

We were both new at this full-time job business. When Rochester first came to live with me, I was working as an adjunct in the English department and Eastern College, my alma mater, and struggling to develop a freelance writing business. Rochester had gotten accustomed to hanging around me, and I'd come to appreciate his presence. When I was offered this job, I agreed to take it only if I could bring him to work with me.

He may be a golden retriever, but I think of him as a Velcro dog. He likes to stick to me. Maybe it's because his first owner, my next-door-neighbor, was murdered, and he's afraid that I might leave him, too.

Mike MacCormac, the director of alumni relations, agreed to my request because he was a dog lover himself, and because it wasn't easy to find someone with my unique combination of writing skills and computer ability who was willing to work short-term for a not-quite-so-generous salary and some reasonable health benefits.

In two days, Eastern was going to launch a $500 million capital campaign to fund new construction, scholarships, and faculty chairs. Though my public relations job was only temporary, for the winter term, I was hoping to move into a permanent position with the campaign if Mike liked my work.

As I was finishing the press release, Mike stuck his head in my office door, holding a cup of coffee. "Hey Steve, did you get back the proofs for the program yet?"

Mike typified the no-neck monster stereotype of college athletes. He was thick-set and muscular, with dark hair and a heavy five o'clock shadow, even early in the morning. At thirty-five, he was seven years younger than I was, though shorter and stockier.

"Just came in from the printer," I said. "They misspelled President Babson's name, but I already called and had them correct it."

On his way to my desk, he stopped to scratch behind Rochester's ears. "My Rottweilers would eat you up, Rochester," he said. "You're too sweet."

I was jealous to see Rochester look up at him with doggy adoration. But I knew that the moment I called the dog to me, he'd be all over me, slobbering on my slacks, shedding on my chair, and keeping me from getting any work done.

I watched Mike read the page proofs, waiting for him to reach the section on the keynote speaker. He lifted the cup to his lips and I said, "Don't!"

He looked up at me, then back down at the page proofs, then burst into laughter. "Keynote speaker: President John William Baboon?" He laughed so hard that the coffee in his cup threatened to spill over as his hand shook.

"Thought you'd want to see them misspell Babson yourself," I said. "I couldn't let you get some coffee in your mouth, though."

"Appreciate that."

Mike had been a football star at Eastern, then assistant coach, then director of athletics. He'd only been the chief fund-raiser for a year or two, and I knew he was depending on the success of the fund-raising

4

campaign to keep his job. I had a lot at stake, too; I needed a permanent gig, if only to keep a roof over my head and Rochester's and food on my table and in his bowl.

Mike returned the page proofs to my desk. "I need a favor. Can you run down to the printers and pick these up? We're going to need them at four to start stuffing packets. We're setting up an assembly line in the ballroom."

Each guest was to receive a folder with information on Eastern and the capital campaign. I had written a series of flyers on critical areas in need of funding—the science labs, the music building, and so on. Every guest would receive a no-skid pad for the back of a cell phone, embossed with the Eastern logo, along with contribution forms and a host of other materials.

"Sure. I'll head down there around 3:30 and pick them up."

He stopped by the door on his way out. "With winter break this place is pretty empty, but I've rounded up every kid I could find and commandeered every staff member who didn't have a good excuse. I've even got campus security roped in."

Mike's mention of campus security reminded me of my own past with law enforcement, as so many things did.

I served a short prison sentence in California for computer hacking, which led in no small part to the failure of my marriage. When I was discharged on parole, I returned to my hometown, Stewart's Crossing, just down the Delaware River from Eastern.

I moved into a townhouse my late father had left to me and met my next-door neighbor, Caroline Kelly, and her golden retriever, Rochester. She was killed while walking Rochester, and my high school friend Rick Stemper was the investigating detective in her case. As a favor I agreed to take care of Rochester for a few days after her death.

He quickly won me over, and he and I helped the police figure out who killed Caroline. My ex-wife and I had tried twice to have a child, but she miscarried both

5

times. A psychologist might have said that I was replacing those two lost children with Rochester, but all I knew was that I liked having the big, goofy guy around.

After I checked my press release one more time, then emailed it to my list of media contacts, I walked over to where Rochester dozed, and sat down cross-legged next to him. He leaned up and put his big golden head in my lap. I scratched under his chin and behind his ears, and he wiggled around and stretched his legs.

"Who's a good boy?" I asked, leaning down to bury my head in the soft fur of his neck. "Who's Daddy's good boy?"

He sat up and put his front paws on my shoulders, licking my face, as I laughed and tried to wiggle away.

"Hate to interrupt your love fest, but we need to talk about Bob Moran. " I looked up and saw Mike in my doorway again, accompanied by Sally Marston, the assistant director of admissions.

"Sorry," I said, jumping up in embarrassment. "Just taking a puppy break. What can I do for you?"

Mike and Sally came in and sat down across from my desk. She was a slim twenty-four-year-old, the kind of girl who'd looked like she had played field hockey in high school and college. Her normal attire was a Fair Isle sweater and a kilt with a big safety pin in the side.

"Bob Moran is a wealthy alum I have targeted for a major gift for the campaign," Mike said. "He's a continuous giver with a strong connection to Eastern."

He looked over at Sally.

"He also has a seventeen-year-old son who applied for early decision," she said. "A legacy kid like Marty who has a decent background gets right in, but his SAT scores are way down on the chart, and he's barely breaking a C average at his prep school. So Joe turned him down for early decision and moved him into the regular applicant pool, where he has even less chance of getting in."

Joe Dagorian was the director of admissions, Sally's boss. "There's the problem," Mike said. "Joe refuses to admit Marty, which is going to kill any chance we have of getting a gift from his father."

6

"You have to understand Joe's position," Sally said. "I've met Marty. He's sullen and uncommunicative and there may even be something wrong with him mentally. He just doesn't belong here."

"But his father is determined that he go here," Mike said. "He even offered to make a $100,000 donation to kick off the capital campaign if Marty gets an acceptance letter." He turned to Sally. "Can you do an end run around him and send out the acceptance letter yourself?"

"You know I can't do that," Sally said. "He's my boss. I'd lose my job."

"Is Moran on your RSVP list for the party?" Mike asked me.

I flipped through the list. "Yup."

"Well, it would be great if we could announce that hundred-grand gift. " He looked at me. "You have a good relationship with Joe, Steve. Can you talk to him?"

That was not something I wanted to do, but Mike was my boss. "Sure. I'll go look for him right now." I gave Rochester a treat and told him to stay put, and walked down the hall to Joe's office.

Joe was, in large part, the reason I'd gone to Eastern. When I was a high school senior, years before, and he was the director of admissions, he had convinced me to come to Eastern over the other schools where I could have gone. I had always appreciated the interest he took in me.

But working with him was a different story. He was only a step away from retirement, and he was as set in his ways as if his feet had been encased in concrete. He was a short, stubby man with iron-gray hair and a stomach that entered a room long before the rest of him. Yet he was as much a part of Eastern as the broad lawn in front of Fields Hall, the Victorian stone mansion that had once been the home of Eastern's founder. His devotion to the school overshadowed everything else.

He was sitting in his office staring at his computer screen. "Biggest mistake we ever made, going to online applications," he said to me as I walked in. "Nothing beats having a piece of paper in front of you when it comes to evaluating an applicant."

"That's progress, Joe," I said, sitting down across from him. I was still having a little trouble calling him by his first name, after four college years of calling him Mr. Dagorian. "Every other college has gone that way. If we didn't kids wouldn't bother to apply."

"So they say," Joe said. "What can I do for you, Steve?"

"Mike asked me to talk to you about Marty Moran."

"Admission at Eastern College is not for sale. Every student competes on his or her own merits."

Joe had been able to keep admissions standards high and he'd been able to prevent anyone from tampering with the way he did his job, because the applications kept rolling in from the nation's best and brightest. "If it ain't broke, don't fix it," was his favorite saying.

"I agree. But every student is unique, right? I remember when you took me under your wing when I was graduating from high school. I didn't know anything about applying to college, and you helped me through it all. I wouldn't be here today if it wasn't for you."

"You had the academic qualifications to be an Eastern student. Marty Moran does not."

"We don't know that for sure," I said. "Sure, he hasn't tested well, and he hasn't performed well in high school. But it could be that he just needs someone to take an interest in him, the way you did with me."

He shook his head. "You do have the gift of gab, Steve Levitan. I'll give you that. But you're not going to convince me."

"Have you met his father? Bob Moran?"

"Many times. The man's an egotistical bully."

"Exactly my point. How can a kid blossom with a father like that? He needs a nurturing environment, the kind that Eastern provides."

Joe frowned at me. "Your affection for this kid wouldn't have anything to do with the hundred grand his father has promised Mike's foolish campaign, would it?"

"Of course it would, Joe. Think of what that money could do for Eastern. I love this college just as much as you do, but I recognize we have problems. Have you been in the science labs lately? They're still using equipment from the 1970s. And the dorms could use some refurbishing. I could write you a list of things we could use that money for. Hell, I *have* written those lists."

"No promises." Joe frowned. "But I'll look over his application once more."

"That's all I can ask. Thanks, Joe."

I did like Joe, even though he was the kind of old dinosaur who lumbers around complaining about how different things are and getting in the way of change. A lot of people don't like that, particularly if they're pushing to have things changed. But as I had told him, I recognized the affection he had for Eastern, and saw the same thing in myself.

If anything, the only thing I cared about more than Eastern, and keeping my job there, was Rochester. When I got back to my office he was so glad to see me that I felt warmth creeping through my body, despite the cold weather outside and the cool temperatures inside Fields Hall. The fact that he was jumping all over me helped with that, too.

It was 3:30 by then, and I wrestled Rochester into submission long enough to fasten his leash. It was a sunny February day with just a few clouds scattering the light blue sky, and he was excited to get outdoors. We got into my old BMW sedan and I drove down the hill into Leighville, the small town that clusters around the base of the college.

The north-south streets, the ones that parallel the Delaware River, are named for trees, while the east-west ones are named after generals of the Revolutionary War. E-Z Quick Printers was located at the corner of Beech and Howe, in a run-down neighborhood at the north end of town. I parked in front of the office and left the windows down a bit for Rochester.

I began ferrying boxes out of the printer's to the trunk of the BMW, leaving it propped open. I was getting the last of the five boxes from the clerk when I heard Rochester barking his head off. I grabbed the box and hurried outside.

A disheveled man was standing behind the BMW staring at the boxes in the trunk. He had an electric screwdriver with the back panel off so I could see there was no battery inside, and he kept putting it up to his head and listening, as if he thought it was a cell phone.

"Just paper," I said. "Nothing worth stealing."

"Wasn't going to steal it." The screwdriver slipped in his hand so he was holding it straight ahead of him in a menacing gesture.

I took in his posture, the way he gripped that screwdriver like a weapon, the empty look in his eyes. In a heartbeat, I was back in prison again, standing in the exercise yard. I had learned fast not to show any fear or vulnerability, because that would make me a target. Neither did I want to seem to aggressive, making promises with my mouth that my body couldn't follow through on.

Most important was that I had to learn how to act, rather than react. I couldn't stand there and wait to see if this guy became a threat to me or to Rochester.

"Away from the car. Now," I said, in my most commanding voice, one I had begun using in prison and polished in the classroom. Rochester was still barking like mad, so I added, "Or I'll sic the dog on you."

The Grace of God

It was like I'd flipped some kind of switch in the homeless guy. He stuffed his screwdriver in his pocket and backed away. Though my heart was pounding, I stepped toward him, physically forcing him even farther back. I dropped the last box in the trunk and closed it.

The man walked around the front of the car, to stand on the curb looking at Rochester, who kept on barking. "Dog isn't very friendly, is he?"

"He's a good boy." I forced myself not to hurry around the car, or to break eye contact with the homeless man until I slid into the driver's seat. As soon as I was beside him, Rochester stopped barking.

"It's OK," I said, putting the car in drive and then stroking Rochester's head as we pulled out. "You're a good watchdog."

He gave one last bark toward the man, then settled back on the seat, and my adrenaline level began to drop.

For a small town, Leighville had more than its share of homeless men and women. Some of the students were easy marks, and there were lots of college dumpsters around. I thought I might have seen that guy hanging around the campus sometimes, but I wasn't sure.

It was scary the way my prison training had popped up at the first sign of conflict. I wasn't sure if that was a good thing or not. I'd spent the last year trying to put everything behind me—Mary's miscarriages, the divorce, my unfortunate incarceration. But thinking I could forget about it all was a foolish idea.

Back up at campus, I parked once again behind Fields Hall and took Rochester to my office. Then I began ferrying the printer's boxes to the ballroom.

Though the old building had been renovated a few times, the ballroom was kept as it had been in the 1850s, with high ceilings and elaborate chandeliers, swagged curtains and a polished parquet floor. It was

11

still used for faculty meetings, concerts and other events. In two days it would be the main venue for our campaign launch party. But for now it was a scene of organized chaos, with long folding tables laden with printed materials lining the walls. I joined the line and spent the next hour assembling packets. By the time I was done it was time to pick up Rochester and go home.

"Things are only going to get crazier over the next couple of days, Rochester," I said, turning onto the River Road toward Stewart's Crossing. "I still have a million things to finish before the launch party."

He didn't say anything. But it didn't matter; I just liked having him as a sounding board.

If I had to pinpoint the one thing I missed most from my married life, I'd say it was the chance to talk to somebody else about my day. Mary and I had eaten dinner together most nights, sharing complaints and inspirations. Toward the end of our marriage, when she was deep into depression over her miscarriages, I felt like I had lost more than just those two babies; I'd lost the person I was most connected to in the world.

Rochester had become my substitute. In exchange for a warm place to sleep, food, treats and care, he gave me unconditional love. He was always there when I worried about job prospects, meetings with my parole officer, or the general loneliness of single life. He sat curled on the seat next to me, listening, as we drove through the dark night back to our welcoming little townhouse.

He had a quick pee, and then we went inside. "I'm not complaining, you understand," I said, as he sat on his haunches watching me prepare his dinner. "Despite everything, I'm grateful for my life. I met a lot of guys in prison who didn't have the opportunities I had—a pair of loving parents, a stable home environment, a reasonably high IQ and the ability to use it."

I put down his bowl of chow, topped with a dollop of canned pumpkin to keep him regular, and started fixing my own dinner.

Rochester was a big part of my rehabilitation. When I came back to Bucks County, I was hiding behind

12

emotional walls I thought I needed to protect me from further harm. He had showed me that I could enjoy myself again, that I could love another creature without fear.

After dinner I checked some emails, with Rochester curled around the back of my desk chair as if keeping me under control. Then we went into the bedroom and he jumped up on the bed next to me as we watched TV together.

The next two days zoomed past, filled with party planning and press relations details. I barely had time to take Rochester out for a couple of quick trips during the day. I had debated leaving him home the day of the party; despite his loving nature, he was something of a loose cannon, and I was afraid he'd sneak out of my office and terrorize the party guests with his big paws and lolling tongue.

But I couldn't leave him at home from early morning until late at night. So I settled for bringing in extra toys and a brand-new rawhide bone, which I gave him as the caterers began arriving. Then I warned him to be good, and locked my office door.

I walked down to the ballroom and spotted one of the laborers carrying a huge pile of tablecloths bundled with plastic cling wrap. "Those are the wrong color," I said. "Eastern's blue is a light blue, like the summer sky. These are navy."

The laborer continued walking in the room, dropping the pile on a round wooden table. "They told me blue. These are blue."

"These are navy blue."

He looked at me like I was nuts, and I pulled out my cell phone to call the caterer's office. Mike MacCormac came in as I was dialing, trailed by two football players who were often his shadows, both wearing Eastern football jerseys. Juan Tanamera and Jose Canusi were Puerto Rican kids from Jersey City, both fullbacks, and you never saw one without the other.

"Those are the wrong blue," Mike said.

"I know. I'm on it."

"You shouldn't have let it get this far," he said. "Did you specify the right color to them? Did you check before they packed the cloths up for transport?"

"Calm down, Mike. I said I'm taking care of it."

"Jesus Christ. It's going to kill us if we don't get Eastern's colors right. You know how many alumni will bitch and moan?"

"I know, Mike. I told you, I'm on it. " Or I would be, as soon as he left me alone long enough to make the call.

Fortunately he saw a couple of guys setting up the bandstand in the wrong corner of the ballroom and took off, shouting, "Do I have to micromanage every single person around here?" Juan and Jose looked at me like they were his enforcers or something, but I glared at them and they followed him across the room.

I took a couple of deep breaths. I couldn't go off on Mike the way I had the homeless man the other day; Mike was my boss, and if I lost this job I'd be out in the cold. Just remember that guy, I thought. There but for the grace of God go I.

The grace of God, that is, and Rochester, who kept me sane and made me feel loved. Just before the guests started arriving, I took him out for a quick run around the back of Fields Hall. One great thing about my office, besides the gorgeous view of the campus, was the easy access to the outdoors. If I wanted to, I could avoid the labyrinthine corridors of the former mansion and just walk around the outside of the building. The ballroom was just around the corner.

Even in the middle of winter, the Eastern campus was a beautiful place, but the college hadn't always been in such verdant surroundings. It had been founded as a charity school for orphan boys in 1835 with a meager enrollment, scrabbling for donations from the public to keep its orphans in sackcloth and schoolbooks.

It attracted the attention of old man Fields, a shrewd operator and himself an orphan from Birmingham, England. The clayey soil of the Delaware Valley was perfect for the manufacture of porcelain and tile, and down the river in Trenton, artists like Walter

Scott Lenox were making fancy china to rival the best Europeans, but Fields chose to concentrate on items like toilet fixtures and floor tiles, which flowed out of his factories, along the canals that paralleled the shallow Delaware all the way to Philadelphia.

Rather than create a foundation to do charitable works and revere his portrait, Fields left Eastern the bulk of his estate, several million dollars' worth of steel and coal stocks, and within a year, Eastern left its single red brick building and moved to this gray marble mansion.

The campus was unusually quiet, as we were in the middle of Eastern's winter break, when the students go home and the professors retire to their libraries. Rochester sniffed his way around a couple of pine trees and peed at the base of the marble sundial, and we walked back into my office through the French doors.

As soon as I'd unhooked him and sent him to his bed, my cell phone rang, and I struggled to hear a crackling call from Pascal Montrouge, a reporter from the Bucks County *Courier-Times*, who had gotten lost on the way to the college.

It wasn't like the place was hard to find. Eastern straddled a hill overlooking the Delaware, between Yardley and New Hope. Any reporter who covered the county had to know where the place was. But I reined in my impatience and gave Montrouge the directions. Then I walked out to the reception table, where each guest had to pass by Barbara and Jeremy, a pair of fresh-faced undergrads from the Booster Club, who helped out at campus events.

Barbara had dressed for the occasion, in a scooped-neck black taffeta dress and high heels, with her straight blonde hair piled up on her hair. But Jeremy looked like he was going to class, in a preppy button-down shirt and khakis.

"How's it going, guys?" I asked, scanning the ranks of name tags still to be picked up, and the empty spaces between. "Looks like about what, twenty percent are here so far?"

"Twenty-three point five," Jeremy said.

Barbara beamed. "Jeremy is majoring in math. He's so smart."

Jeremy blushed. "Do you remember me, Mr. Levitan? I was in your freshman comp class last year."

"Of course," I said, though that was a tough class, ending in multiple murders, and I'd tried to forget about it.

"Really wild what happened to Menno and Melissa, huh?"

"And sad," I said.

"Yeah." I was trying to figure out how to avoid talking more about that class when a tall, balding man in a camel-hair coat walked up, and I stepped aside.

Barbara jumped up. "Daddy! You came!"

"Told you I would, Princess," he said.

"Richard Seville," the girl said to Jeremy. "He's my father."

"I guessed." Jeremy handed the man a name tag. "There's a coat check right behind you, sir."

"I need to stay here for a while and then I'll come find you," Barbara said. She turned back to me. "Sorry, Mr. Levitan. Is there anything else we can do for you?"

"Just keep on being friendly and welcoming the guests. I'll come back and check in with you later."

I walked past the tables groaning with paté, fried mozzarella squares, cheese, fruits, stuffed mushrooms, and other hors d'oeuvres, and made a pit stop at the bar. As I was turning away with a glass of white wine, Joe Dagorian came up to me.

"I can't believe this terrible waste of money," he said, shaking his head. "Think of the scholarships we could have given for the cost of this event."

"Haven't you and Mike been over this a hundred times, Joe? We need to spend a little money to make more money. I'm sure this party is going to bring in ten or twenty times what it costs in pledges to the campaign."

"If the campaign works out," Joe said. "You know my opinion on that. $500 million is too much money for us to expect to raise. We're only a small college. We're not Harvard or Yale, as much as John William Babson would like us to think."

He pointed through the ballroom doors to where Eastern's president was spreading his considerable personal charm among a group of wealthy alumni. "Look at him. You'd think he was some sort of slick Wall Street executive instead of a dignified academic. We ought to forget all this silliness about fund-raising and public relations and get back to what we do best. Educating the young."

As we watched Babson laugh and glad-hand, a tall woman, almost my height, came up to join us. She had masses of reddish-brown hair and red-framed glasses with circular lenses. Her exotic beauty was magnified by the 1940s style of her off-the-shoulder dress, in a tropical pattern of palm trees and parrots. She had a black silk shawl artfully draped over her unclothed arm.

"Good evening, Dr. Weinstock," Joe said. "You look quite lovely tonight. But then, I'd expect a sense of style from the new chair of the Fine Arts department." He introduced me to her, and I shook her slim hand, adorned with a series of wire-thin gold rings. She smiled, and I felt a frisson of attraction between us.

"Dr. Weinstock," I said.

"Please, call me Lili. I get enough Dr. Weinstock from my students." She smiled. "Joe was on the committee that hired me. They asked some tough questions."

"Which you answered perfectly," he said. "And your portfolio was quite impressive."

"Are you a painter?" I looked down at her hand again, expecting to see bits of paint beneath her nails, but instead she had an elegant French manicure.

"A photographer. But I supervise faculty in painting, drawing and sculpture, so I've been plunged into all their controversies and concerns."

"Ah, the life of an academic." I wanted nothing more than to stand there for the rest of the evening, flirting with the lovely chair of the Fine Arts department, but duty called. As I walked away, I thought that if God truly

17

was graceful, I would get a chance to get to know Lili Weinstock better. Soon, if at all possible.

The Pursuit of Excellence

I left the bar and walked back out to the lobby of Fields Hall, looking for that lost reporter. I saw Juan and Jose, Mike's pet fullbacks, standing at the front door pretending to be security and I smiled to myself. Then I heard the sound of someone singing scales, and followed it down the hall to the admissions office. Outside the door, I ran into Sally Marston.

"Have you seen Joe?" she asked, pushing the door open. "I want him to talk to Bob Moran."

"Did somebody say Bob Moran?"

The voice belonged to Ike Arumba, the leader of the college's a cappella singing group, The Rising Sons of Eastern. He burst into song, singing, "Bob-bob-bob, bob-bob Moran, Oh, Bob Moran, please take my hand."

Then the rest of the group, a half-dozen pimply-faced teens, joined him, and I recognized it as a parody of the Beach Boys' song "Barbara Ann." The Rising Sons specialized in that kind of mash-up, putting new words to old melodies. They wore Eastern College sweatshirts, embellished with the college's rising sun logo, khaki slacks, and straw boaters that were supposed to remind people of old-fashioned a cappella groups.

Ike was a tall, skinny senior from Wyoming who volunteered in the admissions office, helping Eastern recruit in the Western and Mountain regions. When they finished singing, he said, "Hope you don't mind us using your office to rehearse, Miss Marston. We'll clear out now, though."

"It's all right with me, Ike. Have you seen Mr. Dagorian?"

He shook his head. "We're just going to go outside for a quick smoke. If I see him on the way I'll tell him you're looking for him."

The guys filed out and I looked at Sally. I was surprised that a bunch of college singers would be smoking cigarettes, especially right before a performance. Behind their backs, she mimed putting a joint to her mouth and inhaling deeply.

"The last time I saw Joe he was at the bar," I said, so Sally and I went back to the ballroom together, but Joe wasn't there. We stopped at the front door, watching Babson operate on the room. His wife Henrietta was next to him, along with their daughters, Penelope, Lenore and Denise—or Henny, Penny, Lenny and Denny, as he called them.

"The man's a megalomaniac," Sally said with wonderment. "I'm continually amazed at him. To hear him talk, you'd think the holy trinity was Harvard, Yale and Eastern. No, make that Eastern, Harvard and Yale."

I laughed. "This party's his big show. Look around you-- all these tuxedos, diamonds, the Eastern Strings over there, even down to the name tags and the ice buckets. They're all here because of him. He's the force that got this campaign going, and if we do raise this $500 million it'll be all because of him."

"A half a billion dollars. I still marvel at that. They say it's the largest sum a small college has ever tried to raise."

Across from us, Babson spotted me and motioned. I made my apologies to Sally and crossed the crowded parquet floor to him. He was a commanding figure in his tuxedo and spit-polished Italian dress shoes, a dignified small carnation crowning his lapel. "Are you ready to get started?" I asked.

"It's about time, don't you think?"

"After you speak, f you don't mind, I'd like you to talk to a couple of reporters. The Leighville *Gazette* is here, as well as a couple of papers from Allentown and Bethlehem. Pascal Montrouge from the *Courier-Times* is around somewhere, and I hope the Philadelphia *Inquirer* will send their education reporter, too."

"Mind? Of course I don't mind. That's what I'm here for. You just gather them up for me. Say, why don't you have the Strings play that fast version of "Mother Eastern, how we love thee" as the first dance? It comes out sort of like a cha-cha."

"Good idea, sir."

Babson and I walked over to the small dais set up along the wall of French doors that faced out to the valley. Lights glimmered along the hillsides and spotlights illuminated the back lawn. In warmer weather, the volleyball team practiced there, and sun-seeking undergrads spread their blankets there at the first breath of spring.

President Babson mounted the dais. He motioned to the band, which played a little drum flourish, and then he began speaking. "Since her founding 150 years ago," he boomed, "Eastern has ranked among the most outstanding and selective institutions of higher education in this country. We have enjoyed the reputation of being a member of the Little Ivy League." His words echoed around the large, high-ceilinged room.

Babson was tall and rawboned, but instead of being taciturn he bubbled over with enthusiasm, no matter what the subject or his knowledge of it. He had deep green eyes and dark curly hair that he styled with the kind of greasy kid stuff I had abandoned when I reached puberty. When I recall talking to him as a student, it's the eyes I remember, and how I wanted to avoid them. But the tables were turned tonight and Babson wasn't glaring at me for some college prank but talking from notes I'd written. And his eyes were trained on those rich folks in the audience who could make his dream of Eastern come true.

He paused strategically. The room was completely still. Wind whistled softly at the windows behind Babson, and out of the corner of my eye I saw Joe slip out the ballroom door to the hallway. Not surprising that he'd lose patience with Babson's fund-raising speech.

"The aim of this campaign is to enable Eastern to take her true place among the great colleges and universities of the world," Babson said. "Throughout the next five years of the campaign, and for years to come, we will continue to provide the stellar education that makes us proud to call Eastern Alma Mater."

The audience erupted with applause. I turned to Sally, who had appeared beside me. "Isn't he amazing? He makes me think we might just pull this off."

"As long as Joe doesn't cause more problems. I overheard him complaining to an alum about the wastefulness of this campaign and telling the man that if he wanted to make a contribution he should be sure to direct it to scholarships, not the campaign."

I groaned. "He needs to keep his mouth shut. Or retire."

Sally brushed a crumb from her party dress, a taffeta number that looked a bridesmaid's dress with the flounces cut off. "You know he'll never leave Eastern as long as he's breathing. This college means everything to him."

"His vision of it, that is."

Babson introduced the Eastern Strings, and they played the first dance, that fast, cha-cha version of "Mother Eastern." Sally said, "I'd better keep looking for Joe. I don't want him to run up against Bob Moran without an escort. Who knows what he'll say."

"I saw him walk out halfway through Babson's speech. But I had a talk with him the other day. He might be mellowing toward Marty Moran."

"And the polar icecaps might melt tomorrow." She looked around. "I don't see Bob Moran anywhere either. I hope they aren't off somewhere arguing."

Sally went in one direction and I went in the other, toward a pair of glass doors that led to the garden. It was too cold to let the party spill outside, but we had lit up the garden to show off its beauty. As I stood there, the Rising Sons stampeded inside past me, leave the faint smell of marijuana in their wake. Ike Arumba wasn't with them, though.

I saw the reporter I'd been looking for, Pascal Mountrouge of the Bucks County *Courier-Times*, a tall, handsome Frenchman who was a bit too oily for my taste. We had a quick conversation about Eastern and the campaign, and he promised to come up to the campus in the next couple of weeks for a more in-depth profile.

Just as I said goodbye to him, Ike came hurrying past me. He looked agitated. I guess the marijuana didn't mellow him out.

"We're going to sing in a couple of minutes," he said to me. "You see where the guys went?"

"Toward the ballroom." I watched him go, then turned toward a display of flowers on a side table. Someone had knocked the table and half the blooms had tumbled out. By the time I had the flowers together, I heard the Rising Sons begin singing and went back to the ballroom.

After three a cappella harmonies they led the crowd in a stirring rendition of "Hail, alma mater, we are thy sons and true. " I heard its words, composed by a couple of drunken grads at a maudlin reunion, and felt proud to be back at Eastern. I owed the school something. They had given me an excellent education for almost nothing, had nurtured my mind, body and spirit,

And that reminded me that I had promised to help Sally find Joe, so I went back on the prowl. As I passed the glass doors to the garden, Norah Leedom came inside, rubbing her hands together. She was Joe's ex-wife, a poet in the English department who also ran the visiting writers' series. She defied my expectations of a woman poet-- she was short, wiry and athletic, and ran half-marathons as a hobby.

"You must have a strong constitution," I said. "Going out in this cold without a coat." At least her dress was more practical than Sally's, an ankle-length in maroon velvet with long sleeves. It was as simple and spare as her usual jeans and cotton shirts.

"I'm from Vermont, Steve. We don't wear coats until the weather drops into single digits."

I wondered if she'd been smoking with the Rising Sons, but that really wasn't my business. "Enjoying the party?" I asked.

"You never know where you're going to get inspiration. I've been turning the idea for a poem over in my head, and something that happened outside just might be the key to figuring out what I want to say." She smiled. "Sorry I can't be more concrete than that right now. I have to let the images stew around in my brain for a while."

23

She looked at me. "We miss you over in the English department, Steve. Any chance of you coming back to teach?"

"Maybe in the fall. I really do like teaching, but right now I think I can make my best contribution to Eastern on the staff."

"I have a couple of students this semester who had Freshman Comp with you. They speak very highly of you. And they write pretty well, too."

"Thanks. I'm flattered." Just then I looked beyond her and saw a streak of gold rush past. "Uh-oh, my dog must have gotten out of my office. I have to go after him."

I left Norah behind as I ran out the door calling "Rochester! Where are you? Get back here!"

I ran toward the sound of his barking, but there was a prickly hedge in the way and I had to detour around it. I stumbled on a rock and lost my balance, nearly falling, then slid in a mucky place, cursing the damned dog the whole time.

"Rochester! I'm going to kill you when I find you!" I called.

He just kept barking. Finally I came around a stand of pine trees to see him standing next to a pile of something on the ground. I rushed across the ground toward him. "Bad dog!" I said. "How did you get out of my office?"

He barked again, shaking his head, and I stepped sideways, letting the light from the ballroom illuminate what he was looking at.

Joe Dagorian lay sprawled on the lawn. Rich red blood oozed from a wound at his neck, staining the dark green grass.

How to Throw a Party

I pulled my cell phone out of my pocket and called 911, my hands shaking from a combination of the cold, fear, and being out of breath. I managed to tell the operator who I was, where I was, and why I needed the police as soon as possible. All the while I had to restrain Rochester, who kept trying to sniff Joe's body.

His tuxedo jacket had come open, and the blood dripped down his white shirt, disappearing below his black cummerbund. His face was pale and his eyes gazed sightlessly up. He didn't appear to be breathing, and from the massive amount of blood I could see I knew there was nothing I could do to help him.

When I finished with the cops, I called campus security as well. I felt helpless, and flashed back to when I had discovered Caroline Kelly's body a year before. She had been beyond anything I could do, too.

I knelt down and wrapped my arm around Rochester's neck, and he rubbed his cold nose against my hands. In the distance I heard the sound of the the party going on in the ballroom. The contrast was striking—here was Joe, who had devoted his life to Eastern, dead just as we had assembled hundreds of people to celebrate the college. I felt a profound sense of grief at seeing a man I admired whose life had just been snuffed out.

I was still huddled against Rochester for warmth when a security guard came up in his little golf cart. "What's going on?" he said, not getting out of the cart.

I pointed at Joe, my teeth chattering.

He shone his flashlight toward Joe, and said, "Jesus. That's Mr. Dagorian, isn't it? Did you call the police?"

I nodded. "You'd better get inside," the guard said. "You're going to freeze out here. I'll wait for the cops." He shook his head, then began playing his flashlight around the grounds, as if Joe's killer was still lurking behind the shrubbery.

I grabbed Rochester's collar and dragged him across the lawn to the French doors to my office. He'd knocked open the handle, and I closed and locked it again. Fortunately the door hadn't been open long so the office was still pretty warm. Looking down at my hands, I saw red dots on my fingers. I realized they had to be Joe's blood.

But how had I gotten blood on my hands? I hadn't touched him at all.

Then I looked at Rochester. He had a red smudge on his nose. "Oh, yuck," I said. "Rochester, you were sniffing blood? That's just gross." I rummaged in my desk drawer for some moistened wipes, and cleaned up my hands and Rochester's nose. Then I pulled a couple of tiny T-bones from the treat jar. Rochester gulped them greedily.

I rubbed my arms, trying to warm up. "I guess I should go back out to the party, huh?"

Rochester just sat there on his haunches staring expectantly at me. Wearily, I stood up. "Don't go anywhere," I said to him. I checked the lock on the French doors, then locked my office door behind me.

Back in the ballroom, I looked for Babson, but he was nowhere in sight. The Rising Sons were just finishing another song, the audience clustered around appreciatively.

I was still in shock and operating on automatic pilot, but I managed to climb a few steps up the dais next to the Rising Sons. Ike looked at me in surprise, and I motioned a quick slice against my throat, only too late realizing that I had probably mimed the method of Joe's death as well as a message to stop singing.

The audience erupted in applause for the Rising Sons. I waited a couple of beats before I said, "Ladies and gentlemen." I had to repeat it three times before there was quiet in the room. "I'm afraid that there has been an unfortunate occurrence this evening. We would appreciate it if you would all remain here for a few minutes, until the police and the ambulance arrive."

The audience started buzzing as a siren sounded in the distance, a low whine that grew in intensity. "If you'd all please be patient," I said, though it didn't have much effect on the crowd. I looked around For Babson again but still couldn't see him.

The ambulance ground to a halt outside, the flashing red lights strobing the ballroom, and the tension level in the ballroom escalated another couple of notches. Women were clutching their evening bags, men talking to each other and pulling out cell phones. Everyone wanted to know what was going on.

A pair of uniformed police stepped in door of the ballroom, followed by Tony Rinaldi. He was a detective in the Leighville police department, a chunky guy of about my age with a baby face and a head of thick black hair. I'd had some dealings with him in the past.

The crowd began clustering around the door to the ballroom, and Tony had to fight his way through them, repeating his excuses as he tried to calm people down. By the time he made it to the dais, the crowd's attention had shifted from the door to him.

"Quiet, please." He clapped his hands together hard and people looked up in surprise. "No one is in danger, but none of you will be allowed to leave the building until you have been interviewed by the police. Form an orderly line and we'll get you out of here as soon as possible."

"What happened?" a man called from the side of the room. I recognized him as Richard Seville, Barbara's father. He had his camel hair coat over his arm. I figured he'd been on his way out of the party when the cops stopped him.

"Yes, tell us," a woman said.

From the side of the room, Bob Moran called out, "You can't keep us all in the dark," an ironic comment from a guy who sold electric cars. His wife and his son were at his side.

Babson appeared at the foot of the dais. "What's going on?" he demanded. "Why are there police here?"

"I'm not at liberty to provide any details right now," Tony announced to the crowd. "The quickest way to get out of here tonight is going to be to cooperate. All troublemakers will be isolated to be dealt with after the rest of the crowd is allowed to depart."

There was more grumbling, but at least no one challenged him. I stepped down from the dais and spoke to President Babson as the officers began forming an interview line. I explained what I had found, and that I had called the police.

"You should have tried to find me first," he said. "I need to know what's going on. And Joe. Why, he was one of my oldest friends." He looked pale and shaken.

"I thought my first priority had to be to call the police," I said. "I did look around for you before I spoke to the crowd, but I couldn't find you. I had to make sure that no one left before the police got here."

"This changes everything," he said, shaking his head. "My god. Joe."

Mike MacCormac approached us from the side of the ballroom, and Babson turned to him. "I need to speak to you, Mike. In my office, now. Steve, you stay here and try to keep the damage to a minimum."

He turned and stalked out, followed by Mike.

I stood there, still in shock, thinking of Joe and trying to ignore the fact that this murder had happened at Eastern, where I was responsible for creating a good public image. At the door, several officers took names and addresses, and asked questions about what they had seen. All the reporters were clustered around Tony, badgering him for a statement, and I asked them to meet me in a corner of the ballroom. There were a half dozen of them, including Pascal Montrouge and a stringer for the *Inquirer* who lived in Leighville and occasionally sold a story to national magazines as well.

"You sure know how to throw a party, Steve," Montrouge said. "This'll make page one for sure. I'd like to speed up my timetable to come back up here with a photographer to take some pictures, get some background on the college. How's tomorrow? Will you be available?" His eyes gleamed. "Everything related to the campaign, of course. Excellence for Eastern and all that."

"I doubt if I'll be leaving on vacation, although I might want to."

"You have a statement for us?" the stringer asked.

"Not yet. I'm going to meet with President Babson in a few minutes. You all have Blackberries or smart phones, right?" Everyone nodded. "I'll email a statement to you."

As a group, they turned to go back to Tony, and as they did, he caught my eye and said, "I want to talk to you. Don't leave the campus without telling me."

I nodded, then slumped against a wall for a few minutes, trying to regroup. After a while, I took a couple of deep breaths and returned to my office.

Rochester was waiting just inside the door for me, and he jumped up and put his paws on my thighs. As always, being with him made me feel better. I scratched behind his ears, and he lay down on the carpet. I got down next to him and rubbed his belly.

Barbara and Jeremy appeared at the door of my office. "We cleaned up the registration table and brought you the name tags and lists, Mr. Levitan," she said. "Are you OK?"

"Just spending some quality time with Rochester," I said, standing up. "Thanks for your help tonight."

"It was fun," she said. "That is, until Mr. Dagorian got killed. This is the first time I was ever someplace where somebody got murdered. It was creepy."

"Don't think too much about it. But you should get security to run you back to the dorm."

Barbara smiled and put her arm through Jeremy's. "It's OK. Jeremy will walk with me."

I shook my head. "Barbara, a man was killed here tonight. We don't know who did it, or if that person is still hanging around on the campus. Have security drive you both."

She looked at Jeremy and he nodded. "Thanks, Mr. Levitan. We'll do that," he said.

I turned on my computer and tried to compose a statement for the press about Joe's murder. My hands were still shaking a bit, and it was hard to focus, but after a half hour I had something drafted. I printed it, then left Rochester with his rawhide bone and went down the hall to Mike's office, where he and Babson were still talking about the potential damage to the campaign.

I handed Babson the statement. He barely looked at it. "It looks fine, Steve. I can't focus on anything more tonight. We'll meet tomorrow morning to go over things." He stood up and stretched. "You both should go home. Tomorrow's going to be a tough day."

I wanted nothing more than to leave, but I had promised Tony I would wait around to talk to him. It took the better part of an hour before he was ready for me. By the time he came into my office, I was sitting back behind my desk. Rochester jumped up and rushed toward him, nosing him right in the crotch.

"So I understand this dog is getting into trouble again," he said, sitting down in the spindly chair across from my desk. Rochester sprawled at his feet.

Back when Tony was investigating a couple of deaths in Leighville that were related to Caroline's death, I had tried to convince him that Rochester had special abilities when it came to solving crimes. But he didn't buy it.

"Rochester led me to Joe's body," I said. "He broke out of here and went running toward Joe, and I saw him and followed him."

I walked through what I had done with him. How I'd been in the hallway and seen Rochester streak past, then gone to chase him. "Your office wasn't locked?" Tony asked.

"It was, but I think Rochester forced the handle on the French door." I stood up and walked over to it. "He figured out that he can push the handle down with his paws if he's scratching." I demonstrated. The door was locked, but when I pushed really hard, the latch popped. So much for college security.

Rochester lay on his side, with one paw over his face, as if he wasn't watching what was going on.

"So he just decided to break out?" Tony asked.

"I guess. You'd have to ask him if he saw or heard anything."

30

"Right. You see anyone coming or going as you ran after him?"

I shook my head.

"Any idea why the dog would be out there? Or Dagorian?"

"No on both counts."

"I probably could get better answers from the dog," he said. "Listen, I've got a lot to cover tonight. I'll come back tomorrow and we'll talk some more."

As he was leaving, Sally came in, carrying a big shopping bag full of plastic containers, looking pale and drawn. "I can't believe Joe is dead. I feel so terrible."

Tony nodded to her, and said, "Tomorrow," then walked out.

"Well, at least the kickoff is sure to make the papers now," I said drily. "Isn't it lucky we invited all those reporters, and wined and dined them, too."

"The Strings want to know if they'll get paid for the whole evening. The violinist said it was probably some disgruntled parent whose kid didn't get in." She rubbed her upper arms. "Could you imagine? Killing someone for something like that?"

"The Strings will get all we promised them. Anybody who can play "Mother Eastern" as a cha-cha has my admiration."

"You know, I feel like this is all part of some gruesome college theater production," Sally said. Rochester came over to sniff her shopping bag, and she opened up a container and gave him a filet mignon tidbit. That made her his friend for life. "I keep hoping Joe will stand up sometime, take a bow, and give us Puck's speech from the end of *A Midsummer Night's Dream*."

Absently, she handed Rochester another tidbit, which he wolfed greedily. Honestly. You'd think I never fed him.

"If we mortals have offended, think but this, and all is mended," I quoted. "That you have but slumbered here, while these visions did appear."

"Wow. You know that by heart?"

"I taught the play last semester." I stood up and found Rochester's leash. "Time to go home, puppy."

He did his manic kangaroo routine, jumping and turning around and doing his best to keep me from hooking the leash. I pulled on my coat, and Sally zipped up hers and picked up her bag.

As the three of us were leaving Fields Hall, a security guard confronted us and asked Sally and me for identification.

"Sorry for the inconvenience, folks," he said when we had showed him our campus ID cards. "We've increased security patrols because of the murder. You be careful walking around now. The police have been out back in the garden, but the rest of the campus is – well—whoever killed Mr. Dagorian could still be out there."

"We'll be careful," I said. "Both of us are parked right behind the building."

"Let's face it, Steve, Leighville isn't as safe as we'd like it to be," Sally said as we stepped outside. "Sometimes I get really scared when I'm walking to my car if there's no one around."

I remembered the homeless man who had menaced me and Rochester at the printers. Sally was right, the campus could be scary sometimes, especially at times like this when the students were off on break. And when there was a killer on the loose.

We walked down the broad curving driveway toward the parking lot, enveloped by a velvety darkness. Rochester and I dropped Sally off at her car, and he stopped periodically to sniff and pee. Above us, thousands of stars twinkled. "Such a beautiful night," I said. "It's hard to believe something so horrible just happened." A car with a noisy muffler rushed past us and I shivered.

As I drove home, the streets were still and quiet, but I knew someone, somewhere in that peaceful town, or on the highways leading away, had blood on his hands. Joe's murder was a puzzle, and since I decoded my first childhood rebuses and threaded my way out of cartoon mazes, I had been unable to resist an intellectual challenge.

"I can't figure it out," I said to Rochester. "Why would someone want to kill Joe? And why tonight of all nights? I mean, think of the risks. Over three hundred people, and any one of them could have seen the killer go into the garden with Joe or seen him cut Joe's throat. And come to think of it, if you were wearing a tuxedo, how would you get rid of a bloody knife?"

I kept thinking about it as I got undressed. From an intellectual standpoint it made no sense. The risks were too great. Was the violoinst correct, that Joe had been killed by a disgruntled parent? Who would care so much about sending a kid to Eastern to kill over it? I mean, Eastern's a good school, but despite what Babson believes it's not exactly Harvard.

Then again, if you wanted lots of other suspects, a big party was just the ticket. Ample opportunities for alibis. Joe had left the ballroom halfway through Babson's speech, and anyone who had an eye on him could have followed him and come at him unawares.

Or Joe could have gone willingly to the garden with someone. Any alumnus who needed a private word about an applicant, any faculty member or fellow staffer. Was Joe's death something personal, something to do with his job, or a crime against the college? What if Joe had surprised someone out in the garden—a thief there to break into cars, for example? Or any other kind of criminal? And if I were Hercule Poirot, would I have an accent and a silly mustache?

Rochester settled on the floor next to my bed and went right to sleep, but I couldn't nod off. I kept thinking about Joe, and somewhere around three o'clock I decided I was going to find out who killed him myself. Though I trusted Tony to investigate the crime, I didn't think anyone else at Eastern cared enough about Joe to help Tony out. My job might depend on my ability to make people feel safe on campus again and feel good enough about Eastern to open their wallets. I didn't think I could feel good until whoever cut Joe's throat was behind locked prison doors. Just the way I'd been.

33

The Eastern Experience

When Rochester and I got to my office at nine the next morning, there were already a half-dozen messages from reporters who wanted to get the scoop on Joe's murder. The morning papers came in, and, as I expected, "Eastern College admissions director murdered at gala party" made big headlines.

The college had a press office which handled everything except issues related to the campaign, which fell to me. Even so, I spent the next couple of hours answering and returning calls, often from worried parents concerned for their childrens' safety, and working on a statement for the College about Joe's life and death.

Around eleven, I walked down the hall to the admissions office, where I found Sally at her desk, reading applications on her computer screen. A stack of viewbooks teetered on the windowsill as I looked at the flag outside the building, flying at half-staff for Joe. The pile of glossy books, depicting "The Eastern Experience," slid off the sill and scattered on the floor.

"Leave 'em," Sally said. "God, do I hate viewbooks! Every time you go to a college fair or a high school or a candidate reception, you've got to carry hundreds of them, even though everything in there is on our website. Joe insisted. And they're always heavy and slippery, too, so you can drop a whole box of them just when you're late for a presentation and have them spill all over the linoleum in some God-forsaken high school in the boondocks. Fortunately, Babson thinks they're a waste of money, so with Joe gone this is probably our last batch."

I sat down in a spindle chair with an Eastern seal on its back, picked one up and flipped through it. It was filled with glossy pictures of Eastern students studying, playing, eating, and resting on the lawn. Classrooms and teachers, local hangouts and the library, the computer room at midnight, filled with avid hackers. It was supposed to represent the sum of the Eastern experience.

You never saw an ugly student in a viewbook, or one with pimples. You never saw students arrested for drunk driving, or shots of the campus birth control clinic or the suicide hotline, even though they were all part of the Eastern experience, too. And now murder was another part. That was guaranteed not to be in the next viewbook.

"I'm sure you'll be getting a visit from that police detective you saw in my office last night, Tony Rinaldi," I said. "I'm sure he'll want to talk to you about Joe and what's been going on in the office."

"Do you think I'm a suspect?" Sally asked.

I laughed. Sally was just a kid, after all—barely out of college herself. I couldn't see her cutting Joe's throat.

"Seriously, Steve. They always go around and ask who benefits from this death, and I guess I do, in a queer way. I'm responsible for admissions now. I met with Babson for a few minutes this morning and he gave me his vote of confidence. Of course they'll have to post the position and accept applications, but he made it sound like I had the inside track."

"I don't see Tony accusing you of murder just to get Joe's job," I said, standing up. "All he'd have to do is look around at all this chaos. Who'd want this job?"

"You'd be surprised," Sally said as I walked out.

I ran into Tony in the hallway as I returned to my office. There were shadows under his eyes, and though his khaki shirt was neatly pressed he didn't look as ready for action as he usually did. Rochester jumped up from his place in the corner to nuzzle him as we walked in. Tony ignored him, sitting down across from me.

"You look like you didn't get much sleep last night," I said.

"Nope. You get a crazy little thing like a murder, it tends to keep you working long after your bedtime." He sat down across from me, laying his heavy coat and Russian wool hat on the chair next to him. "I went over all the witness statements and put together subpoenas for the victim's cell phone and email records. Not a quick

35

process, I can tell you. How about you? You get out of here at a reasonable hour?"

"Yeah, but I couldn't sleep too well. I kept thinking about Joe."

"I've been trying to put together his movements last night," Tony said. "When was the last time you saw him, before you found the body?"

"Halfway through President Babson's speech, about nine o'clock, I saw him leave the ballroom. I don't know where he went."

"See anyone follow him?"

I shook my head.

"How about the garden? You see anyone out there, or anyone coming in?"

"Yeah. The Rising Sons were out there before they started to sing." I did the same thing Sally had done, miming smoking dope. Rochester looked up at me and cocked his head.

"Crime scene guys found a joint stubbed out," he said. "Anyone else?"

I closed my eyes and thought for a minute. "Norah Leedom. Joe's ex-wife. She came back inside as I was looking for Joe." I felt a momentary pang of guilt. I didn't want to be the one who sent Norah to the electric chair; she'd always been nice to me. But if she was Joe's killer she had to be brought to justice. "I know she and Joe have had some spectacular arguments."

"Any idea what those arguments were about?"

I shook my head. "When I worked in his office, sometimes I'd hear one side of a conversation, Joe yelling at her about some trivial thing like putting out the garbage. By the time I got back here they were already divorced. They were always nice to each other in public, but I know he still felt bitter about her."

"What time did you see her?"

"Just before I found the body. I was talking to her when I saw Rochester run by."

When he heard his name, Rochester got up and came over to me. I picked up his rawhide bone from the floor and stuck it in his mouth, and he settled down to chew.

36

"Wasn't it strange for her to go outside like that? It was pretty cold last night."

"She smokes," I said. "Cigarettes. I often see her sneaking outside between her classes. And I did mention it to her—she said something about being from Vermont, how the cold didn't bother her."

Tony looked up from his note pad. "Let's go back to the deceased. Tell me what you know about him."

"I've known Joe for years. He had just started in the admissions office when I was a high school senior, applying to colleges. I was in the first class he admitted, and I worked in his office for a year when I was an undergrad. When I came back to teach here last year, Joe was one of the people who was nicest to me."

The phone rang. "Excuse me." Into the phone I said, "We don't have an official statement yet. But all statements to the press have to go through my office, or the college press bureau." I gave the reporter directions to the campus and the name of the guy in the press bureau. Then I turned back to Tony.

"Sorry. Where was I? Oh, I was teaching as an adjunct last fall in the English department, and I used to have coffee with Joe now and then. He was the one who told me about this job, and he gave me a good recommendation when I applied. I really owed him."

Rochester chewed noisily on his rawhide, only stopping when I stood up. "The phone's not going to shut up. You want to take a walk with me and Rochester? I have a few things I should tell you and it would probably be best to say them out of the office."

"Sure."

I grabbed Rochester's leash and put on my coat, and he shrugged back into his coat, positioning his Astrakhan hat precisely on his head. Then the three of us walked out the French doors to the garden behind Fields Hall. "Joe was a guy with a big personality, very set in his ways. There are a couple of people around here who might have had a motive to kill him."

"Who?"

"In the admissions office you're bound to make enemies. We only accept one out of every seven applicants, and if my kid didn't get in I might get pissed off. You should talk to a guy named Bob Moran, one of our alums. Joe rejected his son, even though Moran was willing to give us a hundred grand towards the capital campaign."

"Bob Moran? The electric car guy?"

Bob had been on TV a lot over the past few months, advertising his cars and how far you could drive them on a single charge. He'd had himself filmed driving along the Delaware and going in circles around Leighville, and was talking about a cross-country trip.

"Yeah, that's him. He was at the party last night, and I know he was angry at Joe."

Tony scrawled some notes while Rochester sniffed and peed.

"Joe was stubborn and old-fashioned, and he didn't like change," I continued. "He was always the one who stood up and complained about new technology in the classroom, cutting down on the language requirement, all the kinds of things only academics care about. He argued with a lot of faculty and administrators who were here last night, too."

"Can you think of anyone who might have been at the party who didn't like him? Anyone he had a particular beef with?"

I hesitated. Mike had been good to me, letting me bring Rochester to the office and supporting me when I argued with Joe myself. "My boss," I said. "Mike MacCormac. This campaign is all his idea, and Joe was very opposed to it. Joe thought the money we were spending on the party last night could better have been used for scholarships, and he resented the influence Mike has over President Babson."

"You see if Mike went out to the garden last night?"

I shook my head. "I was running around a lot, talking to reporters, helping Sally look for Joe, keeping an eye out for problems. I assume Mike was working the room, talking to potential donors, but I don't remember seeing him any time after the introductions."

The three of us walked around the corner of Fields Hall, and acres of Pennsylvania countryside stretched

38

before us. In the far distance I could see a thin band of the Delaware River. Allentown and Easton lay to the north, Philadelphia to the south, and Trenton somewhere to the southeast, across the river in New Jersey. Rochester kept pulling on his leash, like he had urgent business to do, and I was getting tired of having my arm pulled out of my socket.

"Don't tell anybody you saw me do this," I said to Tony. I reached down and let Rochester off his leash. "Go run, boy."

"You realize I'm an officer of the law. There's a leash law in Leighville."

"Dogs aren't even allowed on the Eastern campus. Rochester is an exception."

"I'll say. But tell me some more about how Dagorian fits into the college administration. Is there anyone else around who might resent him?"

I contemplated Rinaldi's question as I stared out at the sweet, pastoral countryside, undamaged as yet by the encroachments of suburbia and civilization. Rochester had his nose to the ground like a bloodhound, sniffing a trail around the garden.

"President Babson sets all the policy around here, and he's both the chief academic and administrative officer. Joe had his set way of doing things-- he wasn't very flexible-- and he was mad that we were spending so much money on fund-raising and public relations. He and Babson used to be good friends but lately they've been at loggerheads, though not about Joe's office. So far, we've been getting more and more good applicants and the college can continue to be picky about who we admit."

Rinaldi took a couple more notes.

"You know, I don't think very many people liked Joe, but I can't think of anyone who hated him enough to kill him, either. For the most part his life was centered around Eastern. He wasn't the kind of guy who inspired a lot of passion."

"Yeah, and when you read the newspaper it's always the honor student who was kind to little old ladies who gets killed," Tony said. "But when you get right down to it, somebody offed him for some reason."

I wondered about that. Did Joe have hidden secrets? Was there something none of us knew about that had caused his death? Was his murder a random act, or was he simply in the wrong place at the wrong time.

Rochester disappeared around the corner of the building, heading towards the ballroom. "Come back here, you dumb dog," I called, hurrying after him. I didn't want campus security to see him off the leash, or him to dart back into the building without me.

"This is why dogs should be on leashes," Tony said, following me.

I rounded the corner and saw Rochester still on the trail, his nose to the ground. "What are you doing, you whack-a-doodle?" I asked. "You're a retriever, not a bloodhound."

He ignored me and kept sniffing, right up to the base of a pine tree. He looked up at me and barked once, then started digging in the dirt beneath the tree. "Rochester!" I said, rushing toward him. "Stop that! You'll get the groundskeepers after us."

Tony followed me over to where he was digging. When we reached him, I grabbed his collar and attached his leash. He stepped back, then looked up at me, then Tony, and barked again.

We looked down at where he had been digging. The handle of what looked like a kitchen knife protruded from the dirt.

Administrative Changes

"You can't tell me the dog knew that knife was there," Tony said, as he pulled an evidence bag from the pocket of his insulated jacket.

"I'm not telling you anything," I said. "You saw it for yourself."

Tony leaned down and, using the bag over his hand, pulled the knife from the soil. There were brown stains on the blade, and though they could have been dirt, I was willing to bet they were blood.

"Rochester did have blood on his nose last night," I said. "And you saw the way he had his nose to the ground. It's possible he was tracking that smell."

"Uh-huh. Recognize this?" Tony asked.

"It looks like one of the knives from the kitchen in Fields Hall," I said. "There were a lot of them out on the tables, to slice cheese and so on,"

Tony made a note. Then he looked down at Rochester. "Anything else you want to show us while we're out here?" I could hear an edge of sarcasm in his voice, but there was something else there, too, perhaps a resigned acceptance.

Rochester shook his head and barked.

We waited by the tree for Tony to go back to his car and get some yellow "do not cross" tape and a couple of stakes, and then I helped him isolate the area around the tree. By the time we were finished, a tech from the crime scene team showed up to look for more evidence, and Tony, Rochester and I went back to my office.

"You have a list of the guests who were here last night?" Tony asked. "I need to cross-reference it against the names we collected at the door."

"About that list," I said. "You won't make too much of a fuss with those people, will you? I realize you have to find out who killed Joe, but those donors and friends are all very important to us."

"Don't worry. I just have some routine questions. We save the spotlight and the water boarding for later in the investigation."

41

I thought he smiled briefly.

As we walked into my office, the phone rang again. "Busy today," he said.

"You get a crazy little thing called murder and everything changes," I quoted back to him. He sat down across from my desk and waited for me to finish my conversation. Rochester sprawled next to him, and Tony even scratched behind the dog's ears.

When I hung up, he pulled out his yellow legal pad again and said, "I'd like you to tell me exactly what you did and said last night." He took notes as I recreated the evening, in minute detail.

"So the first people you saw coming in from outside were these kids from the singing group?"

"The Rising Sons. All except Ike Arumba. He's the leader. He didn't come back in for a few minutes after the rest of them."

"Ike Arumba? That his real name? Or some kind of Desi Arnaz Babalu alias?"

"Far as I know it's his real name."

He made another note. "How long was he outside after the rest of them had come in?"

I frowned. "Can't say for sure. I saw a reporter I'd been looking for, and we had a conversation. Maybe ten minutes?"

"And how long after he came in did Norah Leedom follow him?"

"That was a while," I said. "The Rising Sons sang a couple of numbers. At least fifteen or twenty minutes."

We sat silently for a minute while he finished his notes. He stood and I saw the holster slung low around his hips, the billy club and the handcuffs that hung from one side.

"I'll be in touch." He picked up his hat and slung his coat over his shoulder. He jangled as he walked out the door, and I had a crazy urge to salute him, which I am pleased to say I held back.

He must have gone down the hall to speak to Sally after he left me, because around one o'clock she came into my office beaming. "I'm officially not a suspect," she said. "Thank god. I spoke to that police detective, and it looks like I can prove that I was inside during the whole party."

"Congratulations. What do you say we grab some sandwiches and celebrate?"

Sally agreed, so I got my coat and met her in the lobby. As we walked outside, I said, "So have you planned any major changes in admissions yet?"

"Well, for starters, I sent an acceptance letter to Marty Moran. I don't have the balls Joe had to argue with President Babson and Mike MacCormac. After that, I'm thinking of a few things." Sally stuffed her hands in her pockets and leaned forward as we walked down the hill to Main Street in Leighville. "You know Joe never let me change anything around here. Well, I've been talking to Babson for a while now. He was hoping Joe would retire in a year or two and I'd get his position then. Joe getting killed just sort of speeds up the agenda."

We stopped at the Sunrise Deli, where we ordered sandwiches at the counter, As we ate, we talked about life at Eastern, trading the kind of gossip and griping that co-workers always do. Who was mad at who, whose office was in trouble. Oh, and who might have murdered Joe. "I just can't imagine somebody killing him," Sally said. She shivered.

"I know what you mean. But Tony's a good guy. I trust him to figure things out."

I picked up an extra couple of slices of roast beef for Rochester. When I got into my office, Mike's work-study assistant Dezhanne was waiting for me. She was a short, chunky girl who had been in my class the semester before.

I remembered how the roster in that class was like a grocery list—a boy called Felae, and girls named Honey and Cinnamon, in addition to Dezhanne. I always wondered if she had been named after the mustard but had never asked her. She had huge circular holes in each earlobe and a rotating set of weird earrings, usually flat disks in electric colors. Today's were bright red and matched her lipstick.

A couple of dark curls had come loose from her ponytail, and she looked frazzled. "Oh, Mr. Levitan, I'm

43

glad you're back. The phone hasn't stopped ringing, and President Babson was hunting for you. He said the police were terrible and he's worried that if they talk to all the guests they'll ruin our fund-raising forever. He's meeting with Mr. MacCormac in his office now and he wants you to go down there as soon as you get in."

"Thanks, Dezhanne. Don't worry, he just gets excited."

The phone rang and she picked it up. "Hi!" she said. "Um, I mean, thank you for calling the office of public relations and publicity at Eastern College. How may I help you?"

I smiled and walked into my office, where I hung up my coat, took a swig of cold water from a bottle on my desk, and went down the hall to Babson's office. I found him sitting on the corner of his desk, his long, lanky frame leaning over Mike MacCormac's shoulder, peering at a set of figures. His blue wool suit jacket was still buttoned, and it strained across his chest. "Come in, Steve, come in," he said. "We're trying to assess the damages last night caused."

"Before we go any further, sir, I want to say I'm sorry it didn't turn out as we planned. I still believe it was a good idea, if it had gone smoothly."

"No one's blaming you, Steve. I was all for the party, and I'm not going to waste time crying over it. Let's just figure out how to move on from here."

Mike said, "The good news is that we've gotten more press for Eastern than any of us hoped for. And every article mentions the campaign and Eastern's reputation. It'll certainly enhance our recognition factor, and once the excitement over last night dies down I think it'll have a good effect on both admissions and donations."

That was cold, I thought. But that was Mike. At least he wasn't as eager-looking as I was accustomed to. That afternoon he looked more like Richard Nixon after Watergate.

"This is a short-lived excitement," Babson said. "What matters is the long-term recognition Eastern gets." He turned to me. "I want you to get as much press coverage out of this event as you can, Steve. Forget about maudlin sentimentality. Joe Dagorian would have wanted his death to serve Eastern as much as he did in life. Use it as a hook, if you have to. Promise interviews, pictures, whatever you have to do to get those newspapers and magazines here. I'd like to see this in *Time, Newsweek, The Wall Street Journal*, for Christ's sake."

I was officially creeped out at that point. It seemed like neither of them cared that a man had died the night before—a man we all knew and worked with. But I wasn't in any position to criticize either of them. "I'll do my best, sir."

"And get me a report by the end of the week-- analyze the costs of the party and the positive and negative publicity you can see materializing." He stood up and stretched. "I saw that police detective in your office, and the yellow tape out in the garden. Have they discovered anything else?"

My English teacher background kicked in, and I considered how to phrase what I wanted to say, opting for the passive voice. "It looks like the murder weapon was found," I said. I wasn't about to say that my dog found it.

"Suspects?" Babson asked.

Once again I paused. I wasn't sure how much of what I had spoken about with Tony I should be passing on to Babson and Mike, even though they were my bosses. What if one of them was Joe's murderer? "He hasn't told me."

"I always go for the ex-wife in situations like this," Mike said. "Believe me, I know."

He grimaced. I knew that Mike's wife had left him two years before for a coach at a big ten college, and figured that was mostly why he suspected Norah Leedom. Or was he the killer, and trying to deflect suspicion from himself?

"I heard them arguing that night and I saw her go outside," Mike continued. "I don't know the woman personally, but it seems pretty obvious. Maybe the police are too dense to see it."

45

"I'm sure the police will interview her," I said. "Either of you need anything else from me? The phone has been ringing off the wall."

Babson sat down in the chair across from Mike's desk and steepled his fingers. "No, if we need anything we'll call you," he said to me. He turned to Mike. "I hope you're right about the positive publicity we can get out of Joe's death. I'd hate to have to kill this campaign just as it's getting started."

I couldn't help shuddering every time somebody mentioned death. Poor Joe, I thought. Dead, and no one to mourn him. I started to shiver out there in the hallway, and when I got back to my office I turned the heat up and swiveled my chair around, watching the French doors fog up and block my view of the distant hills.

Rochester came over to sit next to me on his hind legs, so I could pet his head and scratch behind his ears. "You know anything more about who killed Joe?" I asked.

He shook his head and the metal chain around his neck clanked.

Owing Joe

Dezhanne came in to my office a few minutes later. "I've got a class at two," she said. "I left your messages on your desk."

"Thanks, Dezhanne."

I returned a couple of class, then wrote a statement that regretted Joe's death, but gave most emphasis to the capital campaign. What the hell, I thought, Joe would have wanted it that way. He was that devoted to Eastern. It was hard to concentrate because so many calls came in, many from newspapers I'd never heard of. I kept thinking about Joe getting killed, and worrying about what Tony would uncover. I knew there were secrets all around the college, and if too many of them came to light it would make my job a lot harder.

I was just printing the release when Norah Leedom appeared in my office door. Rochester jumped up and rushed toward her.

She was obviously upset. Her hair had fallen out of its bun, and grey-brown strands fell loosely across her face. Her eyes were red and puffy. But she managed a smile as she reached down to pat Rochester.

"You have such good light here," she said, looking around. "A poet needs good light. At least I do. I can't write a thing when it's dark and gloomy."

She didn't strike me as a woman who needed airiness and light in order to write. She was a strong, no-nonsense sort of woman and if I didn't know her I'd expect her to dismiss poetry with a wave of one callused hand. She was about five-six, slim and athletic, with short brown hair going to grey and cut severely just below her chin line. She had well-chiseled features and a piercing gaze.

"I've just been interrogated. The police think I killed him," she said, standing in the doorway. "But I didn't. You believe me, don't you Steve?"

I didn't know what to say. I hardly knew Norah. She had been a colleague when I was an adjunct in the English department, but we'd only talked about

47

literature and student writing skills. I wouldn't consider myself her friend.

"Come on in, Norah. Can I get you something? Coffee? Tea?" I made an executive decision. "We have a great cappuccino machine in the kitchen. Why don't I make us a couple of mochas?"

"That would be nice." She followed me to the kitchen, and sat down at the table. Rochester sat on his haunches next to her and she stroked his golden head as I bustled around the kitchen.

"I'm angry," she said. "I'm not angry that they suspect me. I'm angry that they'll stop looking for the real killer until long after I go on trial and they realize they've made a mistake. By then they'll have no chance to find out who killed Joe. And I want them to!"

"Why do you think they suspect you, Norah?"

I poured the coffee into two mugs with the Eastern College seal and motto and nodded. "It's obvious, isn't it? As Joe's ex-wife, I'm the most likely person to have had a grudge against him."

I flashed back to Mary. Did she hate me? Or had she already relegated me to her past?

"Did you have one?" I asked.

She shook her head. "We fought—not as much as we used to when we were married, but we just couldn't change those old patterns. To make life less awkward Joe and I tried to get along. But it seemed like every time we got together we argued. Even last night, we fought. I'm thinking of going out west-- I have an offer to teach and run a writing program in Nevada. Joe couldn't believe I wanted to leave Eastern. It was as bad as when I asked him for a divorce."

"You were arguing last night?" I asked. "Outside?"

She nodded. "I slipped out for a cigarette and ran into Joe. He used to smoke, too you know. But then he stopped, and every time he caught me smoking he started in on me. I got so frustrated with him. I said some foolish things and apparently that police detective found out about them."

I stirred in some chocolate syrup with one hand as I foamed the milk with the other. While the machine buzzed, I wondered what it would be like to see Mary again—to know where she lived, to pass her at the grocery or while I was out walking Rochester. But that kind of thinking was useless.

"Let me guess," I said. "You threatened to kill him."

"More or less. I think I actually said something like, 'Sometimes you frustrate me so much I could just kill you, Joe Dagorian!' But of course I didn't mean it. I promised to go over to the house after the party was over so he could tell me why he needed me around to support him."

I found a can of whipped cream in the refrigerator and topped the mochas, then handed hers to her. "Norah, who do you think killed Joe?"

"I don't know, Steve, I just don't know. He was a good man at heart, and I loved him once. But when I took back my name I took back my heart, and that was six years ago. Joe never understood me and he never understood why we divorced. I can imagine that he misunderstood someone else, and that's what led to his death."

"Someone at the college?"

She reached down and scratched behind Rochester's ears, and he yawned, stretching his mouth open and showing his rows of white teeth.

"I can't say. Although you know, as I do, that Joe didn't have much of a life beyond Eastern College. If he had, maybe he would have let me go a little easier. It's awful to say, but his death has freed me of a terrible burden. I can go to Nevada now, or I can stay here in Leighville without him watching me and provoking me. It's a wonderful sense of freedom."

"He wasn't your husband any more, Norah," I said.

"When two people are married for as long as Joe and I were you have a history between you that doesn't dissolve with the legal decree. Joe depended on me, and I still cared for him enough to listen to him sometimes. I knew that he was desperate that I stay around Leighville, but he wouldn't tell me why. He just kept saying he would need me soon, that I had to be there for him."

"Did you see or hear anyone else while you were outside?"

"I can't really remember. I know it was very quiet. The only people I saw were two older women waiting to go into the party. They must have heard me arguing with Joe."

"Probably. Probably repeated it word for word to the police."

I retrieved a carton of biscotti from the cabinet and sat down across from Norah. "What do you think I can do for you?"

I broke off a piece of biscotti and fed it to Rochester.

"You're friendly with that police detective. Rinaldi. Can you talk to him for me? Tell him I didn't do it?"

"We're not friends. Just acquaintances. And honestly, Norah, I don't have any influence over him. " I shook my head. "But someone else spoke to Joe after you did. That person killed him. We just have to trust Tony to find that person."

I sipped my café mocha. It wasn't quite as good as I could have gotten at a café, but it was all right. "Can you think of anyone who might have held a grudge against Joe?"

She shook her head. "I sat up most of last night thinking, and I can't come up with anyone. But you know, Joe saved everything. Maybe if you looked through his files you could come up with something."

"I can do that. I'll get Sally Marston to help," I said.

I walked Norah back to the front door of Fields Hall, Rochester by my side. "I'll do what I can, Norah. I want to find out what happened to Joe. You know he was a mentor to me."

"Thank you, Steve. " She leaned down and scratched behind Rochester's ears. "And you take care of this good boy, here."

"No worries about that. Rochester knows who's in charge around here, and that character has four paws and a tail."

The Crackpot Files

I took Rochester back to my office and left him there, then walked to Sally's office, which was empty. I found her down the hall in Joe's old office, one of the largest in Fields Hall, with French doors like the ones in my office, and a sweeping view over the front of the campus. Downhill I could see the massive iron gates that marked the entrance to Eastern. To the right and left were classroom buildings in gray and brown fieldstone. A few students crossed the campus, bundled against the cold.

"I was just talking to Norah Leedom," I said. "She says the police think she killed Joe."

"I can't believe that. She's such a nice person. And she's a vegan."

"Like vegans never commit murder," I said. "Anyway, she suggested I look through Joe's files and see if I can come up with any other suspects. I was hoping you might have some free time to help."

"Joe saved every letter ever written to him," Sally said drily. "I'm sure we can turn up a few crackpots with a motive for murder." She stood up and crossed the room to a file cabinet against the back wall. "It's creepy to be in here when he hasn't even been buried yet. But I need access to all his files and I can't keep running back and forth."

She began pulling folders out of the drawer. "Wow. This whole drawer is filled with angry letters. I didn't know there were so many."

She began ferrying file folders to the credenza next to her desk. I picked up the first one and looked at the dates. "This is my class," I said.

"The files go that far back?" Sally giggled. "Sorry, I didn't mean that the way it came out."

"I know, I'm a dinosaur. I'm forty-three. So that means Joe was in the admissions office just over twenty-five years."

"I'm twenty-five. That means he started working here the year I was born."

"And he was making trouble even back then," I said. "Look at all this stuff."

In 1985 they were still using carbon paper at Eastern, and a lot of the letters in the files were on flimsy paper, letters smudged, still smelling faintly of musty ink. Joe had saved copies of rejection letters that had received negative responses, and it was sad to see how many people hadn't had the opportunity I had to get an Eastern education.

"It makes you wonder what happened to all these people," Sally said. "Did they go on to college somewhere else? Are they happy?"

"Hope so. It must be a big responsibility, deciding who gets into Eastern and who doesn't. You can make or break someone's whole life."

"It's not quite that dramatic. Admissions is a very subjective process. Someone who doesn't get in to Eastern might still get into another very good college. And even if they don't, there's always Penn State. I know a lot of people who got great educations there."

We worked through the files, pulling out any letters that seemed threatening. As we the pile grew, I turned to the computer and started doing some research, beginning with a couple of the business networking sites. I put aside anyone I could find online, who looked like they had a degree from somewhere else and a successful career.

It took us a couple of hours, and my back was sore and creaky by the time we finished. Most of the files we still had open were from more recent years, as you'd expect. Those applicants were harder to track down, and it was likely their grudges were freshest.

We ended up with close to two dozen names. The most troubling was a guy who had applied to my own class, named Thomas Taylor. His application, transcripts and recommendations were bundled into a large manila folder.

Taylor's record at Allentown Regional High School was a little above average, his test scores were acceptable, and his recommendations lukewarm. There was nothing on the surface to indicate either acceptance or rejection; he was one of those borderline candidates whose decision rests on unquantifiables like extra-curricular activities or a personal interview.

A short note in Joe's handwriting, on a half-sheet of Eastern letterhead, brought it all together. It was headed "Taylor, Thomas" and read: "Very enthusiastic about Eastern, though seemed somewhat unbalanced. Potentially unstable. Check further with references."

There was no mention of what further checking might have brought other than the red stamp "Reject" in the upper right-hand corner of the envelope. The letters began in late May of 1985 and continued periodically through 1990. Apparently Thomas Taylor had applied only to Eastern, and when rejected, had entered the Army. Several of the letters remained in their original envelopes, and showed a military return address.

The letters blamed everything that had happened to Taylor after his rejection from Eastern on Joe. He had been beaten down in boot camp, made fun of by his fellow soldiers, had numerous run-ins with authorities, and eventually was dishonorably discharged.

"Whew," I said, looking up from the letter describing his discharge. "That's a powerful motive."

"Wait, Steve, there's more," Sally said. "No letters from 1990 to 2000, but then they start again, sporadically, one every couple of years. The last one came in just last month."

"Where's that one postmarked from?"

"Southeastern Pennsylvania. Isn't it helpful that the post office switched to that system. It could be from anywhere in four counties. No return address, of course."

"Of course. " I stared out the window at the rooftops of Leighville. "He could be here in town, you know. Those letters make it seem like Taylor blamed everything that happened to him since 1985 on Joe. That gives him a big motive for murder."

"He's nuts, the poor guy. I'll bet he never got to college after all."

It made me wonder. What would have happened if I hadn't gotten in to Eastern? Would I have gone off the rails like Thomas Taylor? Ended up writing crackpot letters to Joe Dagorian?

"We should see if any of the names from Joe's files show up on the guest list for last night," I said. "But we'll have to do that tomorrow. I need to get Rochester home for his dinner, and I need to call Tony Rinaldi and give him the list of rejects with grudges."

When I got back into my office, I discovered that Rochester had made a mess of my desk. The guest list for the party had been strewn across the floor, and he was lying beside my office chair with one piece of paper under his paw.

"Rochester! What did you do?"

It wasn't his fault, of course. I shouldn't have left him alone in the office for such a long time. I leaned down and picked up the page, tugging it out from under him. Looking down, I saw it was the page that ran from K to N. There was a big hunk of doggie drool right in the middle-- next to Bob Moran's name.

I looked at Rochester. "Are you trying to tell me something?"

In the past, Rochester had demonstrated an uncanny ability to point me toward clues. Was he telling me something about Bob Moran? But I realized that Norah Leedom's name was on the list, too. And so was Sally Marston's, and Mike MacCormac's, as well as about fifty other people. Maybe he was just annoyed that I had left him behind?

It was too much to think about. I knew I needed to call Tony Rinaldi, but I couldn't face any more thoughts about death. I grabbed my briefcase and Rochester's leash, and said, "Come on, boy, let's go home."

At least I understood his response to that pretty clearly.

Little Gray Cells

I stopped at Genuardi's and picked up a couple of sandwiches, one for Rochester and one for me, and we went home. I hid a couple of vitamin pills in the bread and watched him scarf them down, then ate my own meal sitting in front of the TV, with Rochester sprawled next to me on the floor.

I couldn't concentrate on the TV; I kept thinking back to Joe Dagorian, wondering who could have killed him. Finally I got up and moved to the kitchen table, where I pulled a pad and a pen out of my briefcase. Hercule Poirot would have considered who had a motive to kill Joe, I thought. So I started listing suspects.

Tony Rinaldi had his eye on Norah Leedom. Ex-wives were always good suspects; I knew that if I was ever murdered my ex would be on top of the list. And I knew from our conversation that afternoon that Joe had been trying to keep Norah from leaving Leighville. And who knew what other issues they had between them? Joe wasn't an easy guy to work with, so I figured he'd been even worse to live with.

Thinking of who Joe worked with brought me to Sally Marston. She was bright and enthusiastic, with lots of new ideas about college admissions, but Joe had kept her on a tight leash, not giving her the chance to experiment. And with him gone, she had stepped into his job. She seemed to have an alibi, though.

The first thing she'd done, I knew, was offer a place in Eastern's next class to Bob Moran's son Marty. Could Moran have killed Joe? College admission seemed like such a minor thing-- yet I knew from experience that it meant a lot to many people. It could make or break a kid's future. And for someone like Bob Moran, who had such a personal connection to Eastern, having his son rejected must have been hard to take. Was it enough to kill Joe over, though?

Joe had argued with Mike MacCormac, too. Joe thought the capital campaign was too big, too wasteful, and doomed to fail. He tried to stonewall Mike whenever he could, arguing over every detail of the campaign. Could Mike have finally had too much of Joe's interference?

Another person Joe interfered with was President Babson. He and Joe often clashed over policies, and though Babson was in charge, Joe was so entrenched he couldn't be fired easily. I knew Babson was a megalomaniac, and easily conflated himself with Eastern. But could he be off the charts enough to commit murder?

"There are still so many suspects," I said to Rochester. "I don't understand how Hercule Poirot does it."

He didn't respond. Finally I dragged myself up from the table, took him out for a quick walk, then went up to bed.

Exhausted from my lack of sleep the night before, I dozed off to the sounds of the house settling, the rattles and creaks and pinging pipes that I had come to associate with my feelings of home ownership.

The next day was cold and clear, and Rochester took way too long on our morning walk around River Bend. "Come on, dog, I've got stuff to do," I said. But he wouldn't pick up the pace, preferring to mosey along with his nose to the ground like a bloodhound.

I pulled out my cell phone and called Tony Rinaldi. "I've got some stuff for you," I said. "Can you come by my office sometime?"

"How about around lunchtime? We can eat at one of those phenomenal lunch trucks you've got up at the college." A flotilla of lunch trucks were usually parked out on Main Street just beyond the college gates. When I was an undergrad, they had specialized in the kind of greasy foods college kids love to eat-- under-cheesed pizza that melts through thin paper plates, overcooked hamburgers disintegrating day-old buns, French fries encrusted with salt, and hot dogs made with every variety of meat substitute known to man.

Nowadays there was a kebab truck as well as a vegan offering. But the quality was pretty much the same as it always had been.

56

"I'm sensing some sarcasm in your voice," I said. "Sadly, the lunch trucks go on vacation whenever the students do. Neither the trucks nor the students will be back until Monday."

"Fine, I'll meet you at the Hungry Horse at noon."

I hung up. The Hungry Horse was only one step up from the lunch trucks, a venerable institution that hadn't changed its menu (except to update prices) or its décor since I was a student.

Rochester's bladder was finally empty and we returned home. Within a half hour we were back up at the college. I spent the a couple of hours sending out press kits, answering phone calls and trying to tell people that Joe's murder had nothing to do with Eastern.

Then I went over each newspaper article about the past evening's events, highlighting the good things that were said about the college. And then, because I couldn't resist, I went over my own movements again and again, and tried to reconstruct Joe's. I even drew a diagram of Fields Hall and tracked my movements against his.

Around eleven o'clock Sally came into my office. "I've been thinking," she said. "What do you think Joe was doing outside? He might have gone out there to meet someone. But I know he also got claustrophobic sometimes, and he might have gone outside just to get some fresh air."

"And the killer followed him." I pulled out the guest list. "I was thinking we could cross-reference this list to the rejected applicants." Sally read the names we had found off to me – but there wasn't a single match.

"So much for that idea," she said. She looked at me. "Do think we could have done anything at the party to protect Joe? Put a guard in the garden? Made people walk through a metal detector?"

"I don't think anything could have saved Joe," I said. "But you never know when something else is going to happen. There ought to be more security guards, and better locks on the doors, and more prevention lectures to the students. Eastern College was just a disaster waiting to happen."

Sally pushed back from my desk. "I really have to get back to my own work. I'm totally swamped and without another professional in the office I don't know how I can manage."

"I thought you had four kids helping you."

"I do. Ike Arumba is my superstar – he knows every high school in the Mountain and Plains regions and he puts in about twenty hours a week interviewing too. He's been terrific since Joe died. But there's something strange going on. I always thought Joe and Ike got along really well until about a week before Joe died, when Ike backed out of a couple of appointments and told me he couldn't be around as much anymore. Up until then, I thought he was angling for my job. He was always Joe's favorite."

She sighed. "But I finally went through my in-box yesterday and I found a draft of a letter from Joe to Babson recommending that Ike be disciplined and possibly expelled from Eastern."

"Really? Why?"

"It's unclear. Something about violating the ethics of the admissions office. Taking advantage of his position. Similar high-flown and meaningless language. All I can find is references to a letter from a girl we admitted last year named Verona Santander. She eventually went to Barnard."

"A good school."

"Oh, I can't argue that, considering I went there," Sally said. "But I'd love to know what she has against Ike. Her file says nothing-- Ike interviewed her in Oregon last fall and gave her an excellent rating."

"I have a trip planned to New York this weekend," I said. "I'm meeting with some alumni and press contacts. If you'd like I can give her a call."

"Would you, Steve? That'd be great. I'm so swamped I haven't got the time to do it myself and I'm afraid to find out anyway. Ike is really my best and most experienced interviewer, and I'd hate to lose him now when I'm so busy. I was kind of hoping he'd agree to work even more hours, and eventually accept a full-time position after graduation."

"I'll let you know when I go," I said.

My cell phone alarm played a marimba beat to remind me of my lunch date with Tony Rinaldi. "I'm going to meet Tony now," I said to Sally. "Maybe later we can brainstorm more about the guest list."

I stood up and Rochester jumped up, too. "Sorry, bud, but I can't take you with me," I said to him. "I promise to bring you a treat, though."

He looked up and cocked his head at me. I scratched behind his ears and walked out to where Dezhanne sat, wearing an Eastern College sweatshirt and poring over a chemistry text. "I'm going out to lunch. Can you stay until I get back?"

"Sure. Do you need me to walk Rochester?"

He heard his name and trailed out behind me, sprawling next to Dezhanne's chair. She smiled and petted him. "If you want to take him out for a few minutes that would be great."

I walked down the hill to Main Street. Only a few fair-weather cumulous clouds marred an otherwise empty blue sky. There was a bit of a breeze, which nipped at my cheeks and made me draw my scarf tighter around my neck.

When I got to the Hungry Horse Rinaldi was already there, in a booth by the front window, looking glum. "What's the matter?" I asked. "Look at the menu?"

"It's not like we get a homicide every day around here. It's a hell of a lot of work trying to figure this all out. Driving me nuts."

The server was Felae, a morose teen from somewhere in Eastern Europe who'd been in the same mystery fiction class as Dezhanne. "Welcome to the Hungry Horse. How may I serve you today?" he said.

"Felae? It's me. Professor Levitan. From last year?"

He looked at me. "And?"

Tony snickered across the table from me. "And I'll have an onion soup and a cheeseburger, medium," I said. "Lettuce, tomato, mayonnaise. Fries."

He scribbled something on his pad. Tony said, "Make that two soups and two burgers. With extra onion rings on mine."

When Felae had gone back to the kitchen, probably to commiserate with the chef over actually having to work, Tony said, "You have something for me?"

I opened my briefcase and pulled out the copies Sally had made of Thomas Taylor's file, along with the information on the other rejected applicants.

Felae returned with a confused look on his face. "Do you want something to drink?"

"Water," we both said.

I couldn't tell if he was trying to interfere with our conversation, or if he was just the most inefficient waiter on the planet. Every time Tony and I started to talk, Felae was there. He brought one set of silverware, then returned a moment later with a second. He brought both the waters at the same time, but then he delivered a bottle of ketchup, then soon after a jar of mustard.

"If you say anything to him, he's going to spit in our food," Tony said during one of our brief interludes without Felae lurking beside us.

"Can't you arrest him for something? After he brings the food?"

"Incompetence is not a criminal offense," he said. "If it was, your faculty would have us up at the college every other day."

"I guess you're right."

In between Felae's interruptions, we went over all the files I had brought. "I'll check them out," Tony said. "But right now we're looking closer at home."

Felae delivered our soup and we started to eat. Maybe I was hungry, or the cold weather had done something to my taste buds, but the soup was pretty good.

"By closer to home you mean what?" I asked. "Norah Leedom?"

"Can't say."

"Then why did you? Just to tease and torment me?"

"You're not going to go all Nancy Drew on me again, are you?" he asked. "Sticking your nose into my investigation?"

I pushed back from the table. "I just gave you some good information. I don't consider that sticking my nose in your investigation."

"You and your dog," he said. "Neither of you can resist a good scent."

Felae looked interested in that comment as he swapped our empty soup bowls for the cheeseburger platters.

"Norah Leedom came to my office yesterday. She thinks you've got it in for her."

"I don't have it in for anyone," Tony said, between bites. "I'm just investigating. But the case just seems to get worse against Mrs. Leedom. We've learned about a pending deal between her and the deceased. The details aren't clear yet, but some land in New Hampshire was about to be sold. As the deal stood, she got 50% of the profit, but according to his will, if he died before the land was sold his interest went to her."

"I don't think Norah would have killed Joe for a couple of house lots." I bit into my cheeseburger, and despite the dingy surroundings and our morose waiter, it was terrific.

"Not a couple of lots," Tony said. "Enough for a whole subdivision. Several hundred thousand dollars."

My mind jumped back to the conversation I'd had with Norah about the freedom Joe's death had given her. Not just emotional freedom, I thought, but financial freedom as well. I shook the thought out of my head.

"What about Bob Moran?" I asked, and I couldn't help remembering the way the Rising Sons had riffed off his name in song. "Did you check him out?"

"Steve. You need to leave the investigating to me. I appreciate the help—but it's time for you to pack your dog up and go home."

"Uh-huh. " I noticed that he didn't answer my question, and wondered why. Bob Moran was a wealthy, influential businessman in Leighville, and I could see that Tony wouldn't want to ruffle his feathers.

"Say, I was talking to your friend Rick Stemper the other day," Tony said. I noticed the change in direction but didn't remark on it.

"I need to call him myself. I've been so swamped with this new job I haven't been doing much besides go to work and take care of Rochester."

"See, here's an opportunity. Go hang out with Rick, complain about your ex-wives, and forget about snooping in my case."

"Yeah, yeah." We talked for a while about Rick, about how unseasonably cold the winter was, and a few other things too mundane to mention.

I stopped at the deli down the block from the Hungry Horse and picked up some sausage for Rochester, then hunkered down into my coat and scarf. As I walked back up the hill, I wondered about Tony's comment about Rick's and my ex-wives. True, Rick and I had bonded again, years after we'd known each other in high school, over our shared angst after divorce. But did that reference mean Tony was stuck on Joe's ex-wife as his murderer? And had Norah really done it?

Unexpected Visitors

When I got back to my office, I focused on putting together a report detailing the party expenses. There were bills from the caterers, from the supply house that rented us the chairs, overtime for the security guards and the maintenance people, and a host of other charges. Everything had to be cost-coded, calculated, cross-referenced, and tied up with a ribbon of red tape.

By mid-afternoon I needed a caffeine boost. I was on my way back from the kitchen with a big mug of coffee when I ran into Norah Leedom. "Have you heard anything from that police sergeant?" she asked.

"Let's go into my office." I ushered her inside, and Rochester gave her a brief woof. "I'm afraid it looks bad, Norah," I said, closing the door behind me. "The police have found out about a land deal you and Joe had going in New Hampshire."

"Not that," Norah said. "When Joe and I were married my parents gave us a hundred acres of land. We always thought we'd retire there someday. A year ago, some real estate speculators approached Joe and asked him to sell the land so that they could build houses on it. When he came to me I told him I wouldn't sell my interest in it."

"It's a lot of money."

"It's not the money. The land has been in my family for generations, and I always thought I would pass it on to my children, if I had any. But I didn't, and now I'm not sure what I'll do with it, but I won't sell it. Have you seen suburban subdivisions lately? Awful look-alike houses on cul-de-sacs with silly names. They're soulless, and I won't have any part of one."

She crossed her arms in front of her. "Joe told me last month he was going to force a sale of the property because he wanted to retire early. He'd get his pension, of course, but he needed the money as a cushion. He seemed to feel he would be leaving Eastern soon."

"I wonder why? I thought he loved this place."

"I think he was tired of fighting to have things his own way. Before John Babson became president, he and Joe were very close. John got caught up in this campaign of his, and Joe became more determined to keep things the way they were."

"Why did you stay here in Leighville after your divorce?" I asked. "Why not make a clean break back then?"

"I was already an adjunct assistant professor at Eastern by the time the divorce was final, and there weren't many opportunities like that around for forty-year-old novices. And Joe needed me around. I did his laundry and he fixed things around my apartment and we had dinner together once or twice a week. It was my life."

She leaned back in her chair, and Rochester put his head in her lap. And to think, he used to only do that for me. Traitor.

"Only this past September, when I got the opportunity to go to Nevada did I feel I had any real choice. As a feminist I believe women have as many choices as men do, but I started my career too late. You can do anything, while you're young, but as you get older your age and your own growing desire for security and routine defeat you."

She stood up. "I'll let you get back to your work. If you hear anything, will you let me know?"

"I'll do what I can."

After she left I wondered again if she had a motive to kill Joe. She said she didn't want to sell that property, didn't need the money, but a hundred grand could cushion her transition to Nevada as well as helping with her eventual retirement. I remembered how tough it had been for me, relocating to Stewart's Crossing after I got out of prison, with nothing to my name beyond the deed to the townhouse my father had left me.

I forced myself to go back to my report, and by four o'clock I had a real handle on all the bills and charges. As I was starting to enter them into a spreadsheet there was a knock on my office door. "This a good time for a drop-in visit?" Santiago Santos asked.

Santos was my parole officer, a Puerto Rican with a bachelor's degree in sociology from Drexel. He looked like an amateur boxer, about 5-8, stocky, with muscular forearms. I wasn't sure which of those characteristics helped him most in dealing with his clients.

As usual when I saw him, my heart rate accelerated. If he wasn't happy with the way things were going for me, he had the power to rescind my parole and send me back to California to serve out the rest of my sentence. So far, he hadn't shown an inclination to do that; he had been strict with me, but fair.

"Sure, come on in," I said. Rochester looked up from his place on the floor but didn't get up.

"I see you're using a computer," Santos said, sitting down across from me. "Within your limits, right?"

When I first returned to Pennsylvania and began working with him, he had installed a keystroke monitoring program on my personal laptop, to be sure I wasn't doing any more of the hacking that had gotten me in trouble.

This new job had presented me with a problem, though. A big component of the job description was working with databases, which had been one of my specialties before I went to prison. Mike MacCormac knew what I could do and wanted me to work with our alumni records, improving the data, adding fields and making it more easily searchable.

Santos didn't know about that. I began the job right after the new year, and I'd dodged appointments with him since then, pleading the pressure of the campaign launch.

"Tell me about this new job," Santos said, leaning back in his chair. "What exactly are your responsibilities?"

"Primarily press relations and publicity for the capital campaign. I helped Mike MacCormac—he's my boss—put on the launch party on Tuesday night."

"This a full-time job?"

I nodded. "Short-term right now. Both of us made a commitment that I'll stay through this term, which ends

65

in May. If the capital campaign works out, and I can show that I'm contributing, I'm hoping it can segue into a longer-term job."

"Good for you. What happens when this fund-raising push finishes?"

"It's a five-year campaign. I'm not looking any farther ahead than that right now."

He opened up his notebook and flipped through it. "You're on a three-year parole," he said. "Looks like you're about halfway through that period. You've done a good job, Steve. You've reintegrated into society, found yourself a solid position. I see only bright things in your future."

I smiled. "Good."

"With one warning. You've gotten in trouble with computers in the past, with straying into places and doing things you shouldn't. What's your access like to the college computer systems?"

My heart skipped a beat or two. "I have access to all the regular systems. Email, the employee intranet, shared drives. And we have our own databases in this department—alumni, donors, giving records."

"Does your boss know about your background?"

"Yup. I told him everything. He doesn't know much about databases, so he wants me to be able to pull data and reports for him."

Santos shook his head. "That doesn't sound good, Steve. I'm nervous about you having that kind of access."

"I wouldn't have this job if I didn't have those skills," I said. "It's a tough economy, you know that. There are a lot of people out there with more experience in fund-raising and public relations than I have. But my ability to write, coupled with my database background, got me the job. I can't go into my boss now and say I can't do what he hired me to."

He closed his notebook. "I want to meet with you again in two weeks. I can see I'm going to have to keep a close eye on you for a while."

I wanted to ask if he didn't have any other more dangerous clients out there—people he had to keep from

66

sticking up liquor stores or raping old ladies. But I kept my mouth shut—a rarity for me—because I knew I would only put myself in worse trouble if I didn't go along. There was no way I was going back to California—or to prison.

Santos left, and I sat back in my chair, hoping to coast through the rest of a Friday afternoon. Unfortunately the press weren't coasting and I was swamped with phone calls. Just before five, Rochester looked up at the doorway of my office and barked once.

There was no one there. "What, boy? You ready to go home?"

He barked again. "All right, let me just shut things down here. " I was fiddling with the computer when he barked a third time. "Look, dog, I'm working as fast as I can here."

"I'm assuming you're calling me Dawg as a form of brotherly affection."

I looked up. Rick Stemper was standing in the doorway, and Rochester had jumped up to rush him.

"I just can't seem to get away from law enforcement today," I said. "First Tony Rinaldi, then Santiago Santos. And now Stewart's Crossing's finest."

Rick and I had grown up together in Stewart's Crossing, though we hadn't been more than acquaintances. When I returned home, we met up again, and as Tony Rinaldi had noted, Rick and I had bonded over our shared experience of divorce.

It was at his request that I'd begun taking care of Rochester, and he had become my closest friend in town. "What brings you upriver?" I asked.

He squatted on the floor to rub behind Rochester's ears. "Had to interview a witness who lives up here. Thought maybe I could convince you to hit a happy hour with me."

"Only place around here that'll let Rochester in is Edgar's Emporium. You want to head over there?"

"Sure. " Rochester kept nosing against Rick's pocket. "All right, you get a treat," he said, pulling out a bone-shaped biscuit.

"You carrying dog biscuits now?" I asked as I shrugged into my coat.

"Knew the witness had a white lab. Figured I'd make a friend that way."

"Come on, you're carrying those for Rascal. You know it. " Rick had adopted a black and white Australian shepherd from the Bucks County Animal Shelter in Lahaska. "How's he working out?"

"He's a wild dog. He tore up one of my sofa pillows yesterday and crapped duck feathers all over the living room."

"I told you, you've got to get him a crate."

"He was in a cage at the shelter. I'm not caging him up at home."

"Don't think of it as a cage," I said. "Think of it like his little house. Rochester still likes to stay in his, even when we're both home."

"I'll think about it. " He stood up. "Come on, let's go. I hear a beer calling my name."

Edgar's was an olde tyme drinking saloon in a mall a few miles outside Leighville. It was a nationwide franchise, but it tried to appear individual by using old road signs, Victorian engravings, and mock tiffany lamps. My father would have called it "Early American Barn" decorating.

The hostess led us to a booth in the back. Rochester climbed up on to the wooden bench and curled in the corner. Rick and I ordered a pitcher of Yuengling and a platter of nachos.

"So you're messing around with dead bodies again, I hear," Rick said.

"Not exactly. It's all Rochester's fault. " I told him about Rochester discovering Joe's body—and then the bloody knife the next day.

"He's up to his old tricks, that's for sure."

The waitress brought the nachos and the beer, and I fed Rochester a chip with beef and salsa. He wolfed it down greedily.

"Who do you think did it?" Rick asked.

"I have no idea. He has an ex-wife..."

"Bingo!" Rick interrupted me. "There you go. She did it."

"Come on, Rick. Aren't you over Sheila yet?"

"Sheila? She's yesterday's garbage. Already in the landfill. But that doesn't mean she's not an evil, conniving bitch."

"OK," I said. "Moving on. How's Rascal?"

"He's a wild man. Mrs. Kaufman down the street has a bunch of chickens in her back yard, and Rascal keeps trying to herd them into the henhouse."

"Why don't we take the dogs out for a run this weekend?" Rochester looked up. "We could go up to Bowman's Hill and hike up to the Tower. The dogs would love that." I fed Rochester another nacho chip.

"Sounds like a plan." Rick shook his head. "You know, we're both crazy. We treat these dogs like kings. It's like we live in the kingdom of dog."

"And your point is?"

He shrugged. "No point. Just making a statement."

"What's new with you?" I asked.

"Finally caught the guy who's been robbing houses up in River Heights. Sixteen-year-old kid from Levittown. I got a chance to use that stuff I learned at the FBI seminar a couple of weeks ago."

"Which was?"

"They call it RPM: rationalization, projection and minimization. You make moral and psychological excuses for the suspect's actions, not legal ones, so they're still accountable for what they did."

He drank some beer. "I started with the rationalization. I told him I understand how tough it is to be a kid today—everybody's wearing designer clothes and expensive sneakers. Grills for your teeth cost real change, you know. And you've got to have some cash if you want to hang out with your buds."

"Yup."

"Then you work at projecting the blame to somebody else. If he had a partner I'd make it seem like it was all the other guy's doing. He was in this alone, so I talked about how rich people need to be more careful, you know? A house full of electronics and jewelry without a fence or a burglar alarm or a guard dog is just asking to be robbed."

I scratched behind Rochester's ears. "Are you a guard dog, boy? They say a golden retriever is so friendly to everybody he'll hold a burglar's flashlight in his mouth."

"Not that one," Rick said, nodding toward Rochester. "I've seen him defend you."

I remembered Rochester doing just that, and snuggled his big golden body up against mine on the bench.

"Then I minimize what the suspect did," Rick continued. "You know, it's not a big deal. Just some small break-ins. I told him, I mean, it's not like you killed anybody, right?"

"You don't tape these interviews, do you? Because I can just imagine what it would sound like to have a cop say that at a trial."

"No tape. It's all about establishing a rapport with the suspect. He goes to Pennsbury High, so I started talking to him about high school, what it was like when we were there, what it's like now, that kind of thing. Then I got him to admit to being near the scene, and eventually to having some of the stuff that was stolen."

He drank some beer. "You have to be careful not to be coercive. You can't threaten him or anybody else. And a cop can't promise to go easy on him, because it's not the cops who file the charges and prosecute the case, it's the DA."

"What's going to happen to this kid?"

"He's up at the Youth Center in Doylestown right now. It's up to the DA if he stays there or moves on to a state prison. I don't think he's a bad kid, just not cut out for school and he doesn't know what else to do but get into trouble."

I thought about the kids I had been teaching at Eastern as I fed another nacho chip to Rochester. A lot of them were in college just because their parents put them there, hoping that in four years they'd get some direction. Most did, but some didn't. And then I remembered Thomas Taylor, who had been denied admission to Eastern and whose life had gone off the rails afterward.

Rick drained the last of the beer in his glass and looked toward the empty pitcher. "Another?" he asked.

"What the hell." I'd gone off the rails myself for a while, and though I felt like I was getting my act together again, I knew how tenuous the boundary was between being a solid citizen and ending up on the other side of an interrogation like Rick's. "Can't get in trouble with a cop right here, right?"

"Don't count on it," Rick said, and raised the empty pitcher toward the waitress.

Weekend Reflections

Saturday morning was cold and overcast. I woke early and mobilized for some much-needed house maintenance, which included mopping the kitchen floor and vacuuming the living room.

I had never been much of a housekeeper; it was one of Mary's biggest complaints about me when we were married. I just didn't see the things she did—the tiny specks on the kitchen counter, the mold in the shower.

But with Rochester, I couldn't help seeing the spots on the tile floor, or the fine golden hairs that piled up in the corners. I couldn't count on Mary to vacuum or dust, and I couldn't afford a maid, so I had to clean up after myself and Rochester. Mary would have been so proud.

Or not. The last I heard from her she had remarried, a business executive even more successful than she was, and she had achieved her fondest wish: she had given birth to a child.

The thing is, that had been my wish, too—for us to have a child. But that wasn't to be, and I had Rochester instead. At forty-three I thought I might marry again, but I doubted I would have children.

Thinking of Mary made me melancholy, and the mindless work of cleaning the house gave my brain free reign to reconsider my past. Though I knew I shouldn't, I opened up my laptop after I finished vacuuming and Googled "Mary Levitan."

Mary had taken my last name when we married—her own was long and Polish and had too few vowels. As far as I knew, she'd kept Levitan after her new marriage, though I couldn't imagine why.

I got over 450 results, including her accounts on Twitter, Linked In, Facebook and My Space. Rochester came over to where I sat at the kitchen table and nuzzled my leg, but I pushed him away. I clicked on Mary's Facebook page, and read, "People who aren't friends with Mary see only some of her profile information. If you know Mary personally, send her a message or add her as a friend."

I recognized her profile picture. It was one I had taken, nearly three years before, when we discovered she was pregnant for the second time. Her blonde curls spilled around her face, which glowed like a Renaissance Madonna.

Why was she using that picture? I wondered. Did she think of me when she saw it? Or did she remember our unborn daughter? We had been thinking of names the day Mary miscarried. I liked Melissa, while Mary preferred Rachel.

Melissa Levitan. Rachel Levitan. Rachel Melissa Levitan.

Rochester nudged me more insistently, and barked once.

"I know," I said, reaching down to scratch behind his ears. "I shouldn't be doing this. I have a new life. I have a job, and friends, and you. I need to put the past behind me. Right?"

He shook his head once, and his tongue lolled out of his mouth.

I shut down the laptop and went back to dusting my books. Old books and new books, poetry, novels, short story collections and non-fiction. Old textbooks and dictionaries and dozens of reference books, like rhyming dictionaries and lists of Greek and Latin word roots and anthologies of deathless prose. The books spilled over the bookcases and piled up on the floor in every place I lived. When Mary sold our house in Silicon Valley, while I was in prison, she had stored them all in a storage unit. I paid a king's ransom to have them shipped to Pennsylvania, and it took me a couple of months in the townhouse before I had them all unpacked.

Tony Rinaldi called just as I was sneezing from all the dust. I held the phone away from my face and sneezed a couple of times before I could say hello.

"You aren't developing a cocaine habit, are you, Steve?" Tony Rinaldi asked.

"No, just dusting. Any news on the case?"

"We've cleared Norah Leedom," he said. "Thought you'd want to know."

"That's great. But where does that leave you?"

"We talked to Bob Moran yesterday afternoon. He admits to being outside arguing with Dagorian. Says he went up to the man just as Mrs. Leedom was leaving. So that puts her in the clear."

"Is Moran your suspect now?"

"Can't say. Right now we're still investigating."

"Well, thanks for letting me know about Norah. Enjoy the rest of your day."

"Easy for you to say," he said.

Rochester and I went for a long walk Saturday afternoon, just as dusk was falling. It was cold, but there was no wind, and we walked through River Bend and down to the Delaware River. The cars on River Road had their headlights on, all of them going somewhere— maybe up to New Hope for dinner, or out to the movies, or just to hang out with friends.

I wondered if I'd ever get my life together enough to start dating again, maybe meet a woman to marry. I could feel like I was getting there—having this full-time job at Eastern was a good start.

I didn't see how Mary had been able to jump so quickly into a new marriage after ours fell apart. Had she been planning to divorce me for a long time before my incarceration accelerated her plans? I hadn't been exactly happy with her, but I hadn't been thinking of divorce either.

Rochester tugged on his leash. "You want to go home, boy?" I asked. "Want your bowl food?"

In response he tugged again, and we walked home in the gathering dark. After dinner I put turned on a dog show on the TV in my bedroom, and Rochester hopped up to join me, curling up against the pillow next to me. "Hey, give me some room," I said, pushing against his golden flank. "This is my bed, after all."

He didn't budge, so I scooted over. I tried to get him to pay attention to the golden retriever when the sporting group came up for judging, but he preferred to

74

snooze. The story of my life at that point—my only Saturday night companion a dozy dog.

Sunday morning I tried to sleep in, but Rochester came up to my bed and breathed in my face. When I covered my head with the blanket, he put his paws up on the side of the bed and nudged me. "Fine. You want to go out. We'll go. But it's going to be a short walk because we're hiking this afternoon."

I dressed for the weather, in long johns, jeans, heavy socks and boots, and a long-sleeved T-shirt with the Eastern logo on it. On top of that I layered a sweater, a scarf, sheepskin-lined leather gloves, a down parka and a wooly hat. Rochester wore his fur coat, as usual.

The morning was crisp and bright, though bitter cold. We did a quick circuit around the neighborhood so Rochester could do his business and then hurried home. I swear it took me longer to dress than it did for us to walk.

I carb-loaded, wolfing down chocolate chip pancakes, and then sprawled on the sofa reading the paper and doing the *New York Times* crossword puzzle. Just before noon, Rick pulled up in my driveway and beeped the horn of his truck.

Rochester went wild. I called Rick's cell as I scrambled for my clothes. "Why doesn't the gate ever call to tell me you're here?"

"I'm the police, dude. I just flash the badge."

"Well, I need a couple of minutes to put on my layers, dude. I'm sending Rochester out."

I opened the front door as I was pulling on my sweater, and Rochester rushed outside. Rick was standing by the back of the truck with the gate down, and Rascal was peeing on my rose bush. I closed the door and left them to their frolic while I finished dressing.

By the time I climbed into Rick's truck, the dogs were curled up in the back, nestled into a couple of old comforters he had thrown there. "I know you grew up here," Rick said. "I was there. So how come you need so many layers?"

He was wearing a heavy wool pea coat over a plaid shirt and a pair of jeans. No scarf, no gloves, no hat. "You lose as much as fifty percent of your body heat through your head, you know," I said.

"Wimp."

"Moron."

"Speaking of morons, I had a date with Kelly Kazakis last night."

"She must be dumb, to go out with you."

He shook his head. "I think all her brain power goes to staying upright with those big hooters threatening to tip her over," he said. "She's not much for conversation but she's sure fun in bed."

"Too bad she doesn't have a sister. I could use some of that kind of fun myself."

"Then go on a date, dimwit. Aren't there any eligible females at the college over the age of consent?"

"They're all either teenagers or ready for the graveyard," I said. "I do work with this one girl, Sally. But she's only twenty-five. Do you realize I was entering college the year she was born? Made me feel like a dinosaur."

"The year we were both born." Rick pulled into the parking lot for Bowman's Hill nature preserve, and we let the dogs out of the back. They jumped down and raced around, chasing each other to see who could be the first to pee on something.

There were only a couple of other cars in the lot, and it looked like everyone else was at the nature center. We threaded our way up the winding road that climbed up to the top of the hill, the dogs circling around us, racing ahead and then coming back. Most of the snow was gone, just a few hollows between trees and the occasional covering at the top of a pine tree, like a misplaced Christmas decoration.

When Rick and I were kids, we used to come up to the park and the tower on school field trips. Back then, we believed that the tower had been used by George Washington's troops as a lookout post—but as an adult I learned it had been built during the Depression to

76

commemorate Washington's trip across the Delaware at Washington's Crossing, just below us.

"I'm worried that Tony Rinaldi is going off in the wrong direction suspecting Norah Leedom," I said when we were about halfway up the trail. I held up one gloved hand. "Despite what you think about ex-wives. I just don't see her killing somebody. She's a poet, for Christ's sake."

"Ezra Pound," Rick said. "Poet. Traitor. Locked up for years."

"God save me from a cop who knows literature."

"You have a reason why you don't think she did it? Beyond her being a poet and all."

"It seems like she still loved him."

"And nobody ever kills someone they love."

"And she's smart," I said, ignoring his wisecrack. "Why take so many risks and kill him at the launch party? She could have gotten to him in so many other ways. I think it had to be somebody who didn't normally have a reason to associate with Joe."

"Or it could be somebody from the college," Rick said. "People are always saying how professors get really vicious."

"They make cutting comments at faculty meetings, not cut throats."

By the time we climbed all the way up to the tower, the dogs were tired. They curled up together at the edge of the fieldstone tower. "You want to climb up?" Rick asked.

"Elevator," I said. "We've still got to walk all the way back down to the truck."

When we were on field trips, the school buses would pull up right at the tower, and all the kids would pile out. There was no elevator back then, so we'd climb the curving staircase, peering out through the slits in the walls, then crowd into the observation deck at the top.

Now there was an elevator, which my aching feet were happy to take advantage of. We stepped out on to the deck and the vista was magnificent—we could see all the way to Trenton to the south, the Lambertville and Route 202 bridges to the north.

"So much of this land is just like it was when Washington came through here," Rick said. "Makes you think, doesn't it?"

I nodded. "You think people back then had the same problems we have today?"

"Can't see George complaining to Martha about the way she's been looking at Tom Jefferson," Rick said. "Or John Adams telling John Quincy to stay off the Xbox and get some exercise. But people have been jealous as long as they've been human, they've been stealing stuff and hurting other people and committing rape and murder and everything else the commandments told us not to."

"Spoken like a cop," I said.

"We are who we are."

Walking down the curving staircase, peering occasionally through the slit windows at the green, brown and occasionally white landscape of the park, I wondered about that. Was I doomed to be who I was for the rest of my life? And was that a good thing or a bad thing?"

The dogs jumped up when we emerged from the tower, welcoming us as if we'd been gone for years. They raced around in circles, jumped on us, barked and rolled around in the patches of snow just beyond the tower. I had the urge to join them, lying on my back and making a snow angel. But my grown-up self knew the consequences—I'd get snow down my back, get my pants wet, probably catch a cold. So I just clapped my hands and pointed toward the open back of Rick's truck, and called my dog to me.

An Offer He Can't Refuse

Monday morning, the campus was crowded once again as students, returned from winter break, scurried from dorms to classes. I ran into President Babson as Rochester and I were walking into Fields Hall. "I want to see everything that's been printed about Joe's death," Babson said. "Put a file together for me to read. Get it to me by the end of the day."

I had just walked into my office when Rinaldi called. "Thanks for the tip on that guy who kept sending the letters to Eastern. We found him yesterday and brought him in for questioning. He really had it in for Dagorian, and the college. He hasn't admitted to the killing, but he has no alibi. We're going to keep working on him."

That was good news. I sent a quick email to the President and to Mike, though I cautioned that we would have to wait for an official statement from the police before we could comment to the press.

With the weight of Joe's murder off my mind, I began to look through a folder of newspaper and magazine clippings Dezhanne had assembled for me. Publications being what they are, it often takes months to assemble a complete file, but I read through the articles I had and Xeroxed copies for Babson.

The murder always made the headlines, and the first several paragraphs of each story read like a medical examiner's report. But in almost every case, the article continued with a brief summary of Eastern's history, culled from the press kit I had prepared. The details of the campaign followed, and the overall exposure for the college and the campaign was greater than I could have hoped for.

I went down to President Babson's office just before noon to give him my preliminary report.

"You've done a good job, Steve," Babson said. "Without your groundwork there would have been no benefit to Eastern. I'll look these over. Thank you."

As I walked back into my office, the phone was ringing. "Steve, I'm glad I reached you. It's Lucas Roosevelt."

Lucas was the chair of the English department. I would be forever grateful to him for hiring me as an adjunct instructor when I returned to Bucks County and no one else was willing to take a chance on hiring a paroled felon.

"What's up, Lucas? Did you have a good winter break?"

"I did, but one of our adjuncts didn't. Perpetua Kaufmann. Did you ever meet her?"

"I'm sure I'd remember her if I did. Her name makes her sound like a Jewish nun."

"You wouldn't be far from the mark," he said. "She was a nun, a long time ago. Then she left the convent, taught English in El Salvador, and married a psychiatrist who was working for a human rights organization. I don't remember which one. I'm sure I used to know."

Lucas had a tendency to ramble from topic to topic. Behind his back, his students called him The Wandering Jew.

I looked at the pile of papers on my desk as Lucas continued to witter on about Perpetua Kaufman. "Sorry, Lucas, but is there a point to this?" I finally asked.

"Oh, dear, I've done it again. Lost my train of thought. Poor Perpetua. Had a faulty space heater and died of carbon monoxide poisoning over the winter break."

"And you want me to ..." I paused. "Write a biography of her or something?"

"Oh, no, I was hoping you could take over one of her classes. She was teaching professional and technical writing on Mondays and Wednesdays at three."

"I'm working full time in the alumni relations office, Lucas. I don't think I can get away."

"I already cleared it with John William Babson," Lucas said. "You'd be doing me, the English department, and Eastern College a great favor if you could pick this class up."

80

"When you put it that way." I didn't bother to finish by saying, "I can't exactly refuse," but that's what I was thinking.

"Excellent. Candace has the text and a copy of the syllabus for you," he said, referring to the department secretary, the perpetually sour Candace "Don't call me Candy" Kane. "Must dash. Thanks ever so."

He hung up before I could protest. I shrugged, pulled on my coat, and walked over to Blair Hall, the home of the English department. I found Candace at her desk, surrounded by spider plants in clay pots. She's a Wiccan whose love for the natural world exceeds any tiny bit of affection she might harbor for humans. She was a slim blonde in her forties, wearing an incongruous pink sweater with a smiling snowman on it.

"Here's the book," she said, handing me a spiral-bound handbook. "And the syllabus, the course roster, and a copy our department policies regarding adjunct staff. Fill out pages 1-25 and include copies of your undergraduate and graduate transcripts. You'll have to go online and take the sexual harassment tutorial, register for a staff ID card, and go to the campus safety department for a temporary parking permit."

"Candace, I taught here all last year. I've already done all this."

She looked up at me. It was like I'd said I was from the planet Al'Teresha, and my people taught using fish skins and wooden dice. "Oh," she said.

I looked at the syllabus. "This class meets today?"

She took back all the paperwork except the syllabus and the roster. "You won't be needing any of this, then," she said.

"Candace. Today?"

"If that's what the syllabus says. " Her phone rang and she answered. It was obvious from her body language that I was dismissed.

I walked back across the quad to Fields Hall, sticking to the well-trod if somewhat slushy paths. A few dirty piles of old snow nestled around the bases of the pine trees in dirty clumps. Stapled flyers fluttered from the notice board in the center of the quad as I walked past.

I hadn't taught professional and technical writing for years, since I was a newly-minted MA in New York scrabbling for any work that came my way, but I'd been writing memos, letters, resumes, reports and presentations for years.

The syllabus was pretty straightforward. The class met in one of the computer-equipped classrooms in Blair Hall and students did both in-class and online work, using a software program I had begun using in the previous term. I logged in and looked at the materials Perpetua had assembled, ignoring the messy pile of papers and phone messages on my desk.

Fortunately she had prepared a series of video lectures on each topic. I was surprised to see how old she was—she looked like she'd been a nun when Martin Luther was posting his ninety-five theses on that church door in Wittenberg. I didn't understand how someone could look so old, frail and munchkin-like and still be alive. But then again, she wasn't any more.

I grabbed a hoagie from one of the trucks for lunch and went back to my regular work. I pulled bits of roast beef out of my sandwich and fed them to Rochester as I made phone calls and answered email.

Just before two Dezhanne came in for her work-study shift. "I'm rethinking this whole pre-med thing," she said, dropping a couple of huge texts on the reception desk outside my office. "Do you believe how much reading we have to do for organic chemistry?"

"When was the last time you saw a doctor, Dezhanne?"

She cocked her blonde head the way Rochester did when I said something to him that he didn't understand, but she said, "I still go to my pediatrician back home. I guess it was like, in August, just before I came back to campus."

"And wouldn't you want him to know everything about whatever might be wrong with you?"

"Well, sure."

"Don't you think he had to study organic chemistry? And understand everything?"

"He's like a hundred years old," she said. "And he has a hunchback."

"Probably from carrying around heavy textbooks," I said. "You have to accept the responsibility that comes with whatever career you choose, Dezhanne. You want to be a doctor? You have to be the absolute best doctor you can be, because people will depend on you to heal them or keep them healthy."

"But it's so hard."

"If it wasn't hard, then anybody could be a doctor. Would you want a doctor to treat you, or your family, who didn't have the brains and the determination to study organic chemistry?"

"Fine," she said. "But just for the record, I hate alkyl halides."

I didn't even know what those were, but I said, "Duly noted. " Then I walked back to Blair Hall. Time to be a teacher again.

Style and Grace in a Small Town

The professional and technical writing class met in a first-floor computer lab in an addition at the back of Blair Hall that hadn't been there when I was a student. The rest of the building was dark and gloomy, with tall, gothic-arched windows in the classrooms, and dusty fluorescent lights hung on pendants. The classrooms had rich wooden wainscoting and scuffed floors, and I had fond memories of seminars in the small rooms on the third floor, a professor and a handful of students discussing the meaning of life and literature.

At least that's the way I remember it. We were probably as uncommunicative as today's students, and our professors must have felt like brain surgeons, probing our heads for any spark of intelligence.

Tall windows in the computer classroom looked out on a walkway between buildings, where the grass was sparse and brown. A squirrel shook the branches of a pine tree as I walked in to the room, causing a flurry of the last fine snow outside the window.

Computers lined the perimeter of the room. About twenty students either sat at the terminals or at a couple of round tables in the middle of the room. I threaded my way through them, saying "Good afternoon," until I reached the podium.

"You're not Sister Perpetua," a boy at one of the round tables said.

"That's very perceptive," I said. "I'm Professor Steve Levitan, and I've been asked to take over your class for the rest of the term."

"What happened to the sister?" a girl asked from the side of the room.

"She was called to her heavenly reward last Thursday night. I see from her syllabus that we're discussing memos today. I'm going to give you a brief lecture on memos, and then I'm going to ask you to write a memo for distribution to the campus about Professor Kaufman and her death."

"Will we have to use the phrase 'heavenly reward' in the memo?" the same snarky boy at the table asked.

"If it's appropriate for your audience." I used that as a segue into the topic of memos, forestalling any more comments. I told them how long I'd been teaching at Eastern, and about my current job in the alumni office. "I write this kind of material for a living these days," I said. "And those of you who see yourselves earning a living at some point in the distant future will need to know how to communicate with your colleagues, your clients, and any other audience as appropriate."

I pulled up Perpetua Kaufman's video lecture on memos. She was surprisingly animated for such an elderly, gnome-like person, and I was sorry that I hadn't had a chance to get to know her over the past year. But adjuncts tend to come and go as classes demand, and we don't spend a lot of time socializing with each other, or with full-time faculty.

When the video was finished, I said, "Now I want you to consider the audience for your memo. Are you writing to your fellow students? To the faculty and administration? How do you think your memo might be different based on those different audiences?"

The snarky kid raised his hand. "What's your name?" I asked.

"Lou Segusi. You could change the kind of language you use—more colloquial for students, more formal for adults."

"I'm not sure all the faculty here behave like adults," I said. "But that's a good point. Any other ideas?"

No one else had anything to say, so I started picking names off the roster, starting with one I recognized, the girl from the booster club who had helped out at the party. "Barbara Seville?"

"Professor Kaufman had a really interesting life. You could pick out different details to tell about her depending on the audience."

"Good point. Where could you find information on Professor Kaufman for your memo?" I looked back at my roster. "Yenny?"

85

I expected a girl, but a skinny boy with a wild bush of dark hair raised his hand. "Google?"

"Yes, but Google's just a search engine—it just points you to sources. What kind of source would have the information you need?"

"An obituary?" Lou asked.

"Good idea. You can find obituaries by checking the local papers. What about something closer to home? La'Rose?" I asked.

A black girl with elaborate braids raised her hand. "Maybe on the Eastern website?"

"Yup. There's often information about your professors on the site. " I called the rest of the roll, then showed them where to find the memo templates in Microsoft Word. "You have the rest of the class to write this memo. Use the assignment button to submit."

As they worked, I went up to the teaching station and used the computer there to log in to my email. I managed to answer a couple of press queries before Lou raised his hand and asked, "Professor?"

"Yup?"

"If I finish the assignment can I use the computer to work on something else? Sister Perpetua always let us."

"I don't have a problem with that." I went back to my emails, and a few minutes before the end of class I walked around the room, looking over shoulders. "You don't need the CC: field if you're not copying anyone on the memo," I told La'Rose. "You don't have to put a salutation on a memo," I told Ashleen.

As I passed Lou's computer I saw that he was working on a paper for history class that had someone else's name on the top. "That your paper?" I asked.

"I'm just proofing for a friend." He minimized the paper quickly.

It looked more like he was writing it for a friend, but I wasn't going to start my first day by accusing a stranger of plagiarism. I went back up to the podium. "Remember, guys, I will be grading you based on the format of your memo, as well as your ability to write clearly and punctuate appropriately."

86

They all began packing up. Lou was the last to go, typing away up until his last classmate had left and I was standing by the door. "I'm going to lock the door," I said. "You can stay here until the next class comes in."

"Thanks, Prof," he said, still clacking away at the keyboard.

Eastern was to close at four o'clock that afternoon so we could all attend Joe Dagorian's funeral at Saint Augustine's in Leighville, and I got back to my office just in time to say hi to Rochester and give him a rawhide bone until I returned from the funeral. I didn't want to contemplate what kind of mischief he might get up to at a cemetery.

I rode out to Saint Augustine's with Sally Marston, and we slipped into a pew in front of Mike MacCormac and Sam Boni, the director of intercollegiate athletics. Sam looked like a California beach boy sprung to life from the pages of a fashion catalog. He had been a collegiate swimmer and water polo champ at a California college and he had maintained a swimmer's lean and muscular physique. He also had wheat-blond hair, blue eyes, and cheekbones models die for. A few rows back I saw Norah's colleagues from the English department, and other departments were grouped around us.

The priest concluded his eulogy by saying, "Someone told me that Joe managed a difficult process with style and grace, and that he managed to convey to the students who weren't admitted that it was in their best interests to forget about Eastern and move on to a better place for them. Today, we bid farewell to Joe as he heads to his own better place."

The cemetery was behind the church, and we followed the pallbearers and the coffin down a paved path, and then across to the plot that had been reserved for Joe. A wind came up as we stood around the hillside grave and the priest read a few words. I could feel that chill January wind sweeping across the Pennsylvania countryside and raising our fuel bills as we shivered in it.

While the others stood and mingled for a few minutes after the coffin had been lowered into the earth, I walked to the top of the rise and looked out on the countryside. Before me, just beyond a checkerboard of farmland, lay Leighville, its black roofs clustered together as if for warmth. Below my feet blades of grass poked up through a thin slush, while along the roads it had turned a brown grey from the exhaust of passing cars, and on the far hills it still looked deep and white.

As I stared out at the roofs of Eastern College, I thought about how much the college had changed since it was founded. About all the Joe Dagorians and the Steve Levitans who must have worked there over the years, whose names and records were lost to history. What we remember of history is usually the movers and shakers, the people who change things. The Joe Dagorians merely maintain the status quo.

I rode back to Eastern with Sally, picked up Rochester, and headed downriver. Night was just falling, neons awakening and cars just beginning to turn on their headlights.

One of the things I had to adjust to when I came back to Bucks County, after the bright halogens of Silicon Valley, was the lack of street lights. Where I lived with Mary, the night was almost as bright as the day, between the streetlights, store window lights, neon signs and headlights. But in the country, when it was dark, it was dark. Most nights I found the dark welcoming, a soft gloom that overtook the day and gave us time to recharge. But since Joe died I had started to fear the night, because it covered the evil around us. I shivered and Rochester snuggled next to me.

As I fixed dinner, I kept one eye on the evening news, and saw Thomas Taylor being led into the police station. "That's the homeless guy who was hanging around the car when we went to the printers," I said to Rochester. "I wonder if he picked up one of the programs from my car. Oh my God, maybe it was because of me that he knew where he could find Joe."

I had to sit down, and Rochester came over to press his head against my knee. My mind was full of questions about the contact between Taylor and Joe. Had Taylor been hovering around outside Fields Hall and taken advantage of Joe's trip outside? Or had he contacted Joe and made arrangements to meet him outside? And would Taylor have even known about the party if it wasn't for me?

Living in Fear

I couldn't concentrate for the rest of the evening. I wanted to call Tony Rinaldi and ask what he'd learned from Taylor, but I knew it wasn't my business. I played endless games of computer solitaire, Scrabble and mah johngg and finally took a sleeping pill around eleven, after taking Rochester out for a quick pee.

The next morning I woke early and heard the slap of the *Courier-Times* on the driveway. I yawned, climbed out of bed, and dressed for dog-walking. On my way down the driveway, Rochester pulling me like he was the lead engine on a freight train, I picked up the paper and pulled it out of its plastic wrapper. As I followed Rochester down the street, I unfolded it and the headline jumped out at me.

"Is Eastern College Safe?" it read. "Campus murder has students living in fear."

Pascal Montrouge, who I had pegged as a sleazeball the first time I met him, had interviewed students, faculty and staff members and recorded their fears that lax security had led to Joe's murder. "I can't sleep at night," one girl was quoted as saying. "My roommate and I take turns taking naps during the day."

He hadn't come to me for my take on the situation, which I resented. He pointed out that a homeless man had been detained in connection with the murders, which further spurred questions about campus security. He made it seem like homeless people were camped all around the college grounds.

There was no mention of Taylor's connection with the College or any possible motive, which I thought was a serious omission. It Taylor was the killer, then Joe's murder hadn't been a random act that should sow fear throughout the college.

My anger simmered as Rochester and I drove up the River Road to Leighville. The weather was warming up, and the sun had melted most of the snow in the fields and farmyards. The campus was almost completely snow-free.

90

I picked up a copy of the *Eastern Daily Sun*, the campus newspaper, in the lobby of Fields Hall on my way to my office. The front page featured a story about campus security, and I stopped at the foot of the curving staircase to read it. An unnamed source in the campus security office claimed that the incidence of crime on the campus had risen nearly 50% in the past year. There had been more muggings, burglaries and violent assaults in the last year than in the previous three. Our director of security had declined to comment on the story, which unfortunately lent credence to the report.

As I walked into my office, Babson's secretary buzzed me with a summons.

"I presume you've seen the morning paper," he said when I walked into his office. Mike was sitting in the visitor chair next to Babson's desk.

"Good morning, President Babson. Morning, Mike. Yes, I read the article, in the *Courier-Times*, and then the one in the *Daily Sun*. Is it true? We've upped our security patrols?"

"Do we have any choice?" he asked. "I think Eastern College is as safe as any campus in the United States, but we have to do something to reassure people."

I saw down next to Mike and the three of us discussed strategies for replying to press queries about security. Babson was worried that if the story continued much longer it could have a negative impact on everything we did. "Sally says that admissions is getting questions," he said. "And I've already heard from three alumni parents this morning. We don't want this to develop into some kind of mob mentality—students transferring, declining our offers of admission. Then the faculty start to leave and donations tank. We've got to catch this, Steve, or we could find ourselves on a downward spiral we can't stop."

"I don't understand why the police haven't released the fact that Thomas Taylor had a personal motive," I said. "That should make things easier for us. That he's not just some random homicidal homeless man. I'm going to call Sergeant Rinaldi and check in with him, and then I'll start working the phones."

"Protecting Eastern's reputation is job one right now," Babson said. "Let me know if you need me or my office to do anything."

When I returned to my office, Montrouge finally called for my statement. I wanted to be petty and snub him, but that would only make things wors.

But all I could do was confirm that the incidence of burglary on campus is up, while assault and muggings had dropped dramatically. "But there's no relationship between these problems, which every campus has to some degree, and Joe's death."

"I'm not sure about that, Steve," he said. His French accent had become very irritating. I wanted to tell him that my name was not Stiv but I refrained.

"It was an isolated incident," I insisted. "You should talk to Sergeant Rinaldi at the Leighville police. See what he has to say about the suspect he has in custody."

"He's not saying anything," Montrouge said. "So right now all I have is the problems at the campus. "I'm working on a follow up story for tomorrow's paper."

I struggled to get him to focus on the positives about Eastern, but as he pointed out, good news doesn't sell papers.

As soon as I hung up with Montrouge I called Tony Rinaldi. "Are you going to charge that homeless guy I saw on the news last night?" I asked.

"Not yet. We're still checking his motive and his alibi."

All through the morning, aumni called me. Reporters called me. Parents of current students called, and so did students and faculty members and even support staff from other offices. "Yes, it's safe to park in the faculty lot," I said. "No, we're not planning to give guns to our security guards. No, no one else has been murdered on campus."

At eleven-thirty we all gathered in Babson's office and he opened our staff meeting, as he usually did, with a ten-minute tirade about the inefficiency he had seen around the campus since we last had met. He paid a prodigious amount of attention to detail-- out-of-date bulletin boards, scarcity of recruiting materials in the admissions office waiting room, overflowing trash bins outside the dorms, an untended leak in the lobby of the gym. He delivered yet another pile of Ivy League clippings to me, and a Stanford viewbook to Sally.

Sam Boni was cheerful and cool in giving his report, and maintained his equanimity even when Babson railed about the ineptitude of the women's volleyball team. "The ball goes over the net!" he yelled. "Not under it. Not into it. Do they need someone to tell them that?"

"They know, President Babson. Remember, they're playing for the fun of it, for the chance to compete. They do their best."

I aimed for a friendly professionalism in my report. "Even though Joe's murder was tragic and resulted in some unpleasant sensationalized publicity for Eastern, we've gotten a great deal of good publicity as well. Every article mentions the attractiveness of the campus, the academic strengths of the college and the quality of the student body."

"Murder trumps a pretty campus or a bunch of smart students, Steve," Babson said. "You've got to get these reporters to stop mentioning Joe's death or trying to link it to security issues here. That kind of news does us no good at all."

"I won't let you down," I said.

"See that you don't." He turned to Sally. "How are things going in your office?"

"We've been swamped with calls and emails," she said. "We're expecting a flood of late applicants that could potentially move our selectivity ratio up by several percentage points."

"Even with all this news of the murder?" he asked.

She nodded. "Steve's right. Most people aren't paying attention to Joe's death or any potential safety issues. They're just seeing Eastern's name and reputation, and that seems to be spurring them to apply."

Mike MacCormac reported on the progress of the capital campaign. "Individual contributions are coming in more rapidly than we expected. Corporate and foundation support is also proving easier to obtain. It seems the publicity surrounding Eastern recently has made our name much more recognizable."

Mike stood up and started to pace back and forth in front of the table. "Even with this early support, our alumni and friends will have to realize," he said, pounding the air with his fist as he talked, "That their support is essential to the success of this campaign, and to Eastern's future. We have an elderly faculty, a decaying physical plant and a declining applicant base. But we have a solid academic program and an excellent national reputation, and with enough money behind us we can fix any leak, recruit any student, hire any professor. We can do what must be done to make Eastern number one."

I stole a glance at Sally, and had to smother a giggle. It was like seeing a younger Babson with a darker beard, but a Babson possessed with a vision of Eastern.

"Just as much as any professor on this faculty, we're educators," Mike said. "We have to get the message across to our donors that Eastern needs their dollars, we need their support."

In his fervor he reminded me of those television evangelists whose passion rages through them like a fever. His face had gotten a little red, and his eyes positively glowed like one of the Ayatollah's henchmen who had just gunned down a Yankee imperialist in the name of the Holy Jihad. Babson grinned benevolently behind him. Though Babson had no children of his own, he had infected Mike with enough of his spirit and belief in Eastern to make him as close to a son as he could.

Both he and Babson could be frightening. I was glad that reporters like Pascal Montrouge hadn't been exposed to their level of fanaticism. While it would make great copy to show the megalomania at the Eastern's head, it wouldn't be a good thing for my career in public relations.

When Mike finished, Babson banged his fist on the table. "I want you all to remember that this campaign is my legacy. Generations of students will remember my name. I'm depending on every one of you to make my vision come true."

He stood up. "Meeting adjourned," he said as he turned and walked out.

"And have a nice day," I said under my breath. Sally laughed.

A Nose For News

There were more phone calls when I got back to my office, and more questions about campus safety. Around four o'clock, Tony Rinaldi called. "I wanted to give you a heads up on some bad news," he said. "We got a partial print from the knife, and it doesn't match Thomas Taylor—or Norah Leedom, for that matter. So it looks like he's in the clear."

"What about Bob Moran?" I asked. "Didn't you say that he was out in the garden with Joe, too?"

"Yeah, but he's got an attorney and he's not talking."

"Can you get his fingerprints?"

"We can. But since he's not cooperating, it requires a subpoena, and I'm going to need a lot more evidence before I can ask for one. So far, I don't have anyone who witnessed them talking, and we don't have evidence that he made any threats toward Dagorian."

I walked back down the hall to President Babson's office to pass the news on to him, but he had already left for a fund-raising cocktail party in New York. I decided to wait until the morning to tell him.

Back at my desk, I didn't have much appetite for work. So I gathered up my stuff, hooked up Rochester's leash, and closed my office. I shivered as Rochester and I walked back to my car, and not just from the cold or the bitter wind that had picked up. Leighville was dangerous. Eastern College was dangerous.

I spent an hour or that evening grading the tech writing class's memos about the death of Perpetua Kaufman. I discovered that she had lived in Stewart's Crossing, too, in a little house along the canal, between Main Street and the Delaware River. I remembered those houses—there were twelve of them in a row, all built to house canal workers back in the 1800s. When I was a kid the residents used to decorate them all together as the twelve days of Christmas. I wondered which house had been Perpetua's—the partridge in a pear tree? The twelve drummers drumming? Or some anonymous number in between? My favorite as a teenager had been the six geese-a-laying; my friends and I made a lot of snickering jokes about geese getting laid.

The next morning I read the *Gazette* and the *Courier-Times* at my desk. Both carried the story of Thomas Taylor's release. That combined with the news about security issues at Eastern to keep the story of Joe's murder going. Both papers were full of speculation about the case, wondering if someone on the faculty or staff was the murder, and that perhaps Eastern College was a co-conspirator.

I went down to the kitchen for coffee when I finished reading, and Rochester followed me, hoping one of the staff had left something edible at his level. Sally was sitting at the big oak table, wearing her usual Fair Isle sweater, this one with a big "Go Eastern, Young Student" button just below the collar. She had papers spread out before her and a big mug of coffee at her side. "I had to get out of my office," she said. "Or Joe's office, really. The phone just doesn't stop ringing, and I have to pull together some statistics for Babson."

Rochester put his paws up on the table and nosed at a piece of paper. "You can't eat that, Rochester," I said, tugging him back to the floor by his collar.

"What kind of stats do you need?" I asked. "I did some statistical work in the past, mostly with databases."

"An admissions office lives and dies on yield," she said. "That's the percentage of students who are offered admission who accept the offer. As the yield goes down, we have to accept more and more students to make a class, and the qualifications we consider get lower and lower."

Rochester jumped back up to the table. His paw grabbed a piece of paper and tossed it to the floor.

"Rochester! Bad dog!" I said, leaning down to pick up the paper.

He nudged his head against my arm, and he tried to grab the page in his mouth as I got up.

"What is it about this paper?" I asked. "Did someone spill some food on it?"

I looked down. "This is the report Joe published last year. Wow. We got thirty-five hundred applications last year. I didn't realize it was that many."

"Thirty-five hundred? That's not right." Sally fiddled around with her papers. "Here's the number. It was twenty-eight hundred."

"That's a big gap," I said.

"Let me see that report."

I handed it to her and she scanned it. "It says here that our yield was a one in seven ratio, but the real numbers show more like one in five."

I sat down across from her, and Rochester plopped on the floor behind my chair. "Are you sure?"

"See for yourself. " She passed a bunch of pages to me and turned the calculator so that it faced me. I started adding the numbers for the different categories of students.

I added them twice, just to be sure. "You're right," I said. "Maybe when Joe put out this report he just made a mistake."

"These aren't mistakes. These are lies. " Sally picked up her coffee mug, cradling it in one hand, but didn't drink. "With a one in five ratio, we're a lot lower than the Ivies or many of the other schools in our category. You know how keen Babson is on competing with Harvard and Yale."

"Have you checked any of the other statistics we published last year?" I asked. "SAT scores and so on?"

She shook her head. "I guess we should, though."

We needed more information than she had in the kitchen, so Rochester and I followed her back to her office. He curled up in the corner near the heater while she and I sifted through documents and called up computer files. It was nearly lunchtime before we were finished.

"This is scary," Sally said. "Joe pumped up our average SAT scores a few points and gave us a couple of National Merit Scholars who actually went somewhere else. He even inflated the percentage of minority students here. We're talking serious breach of ethics, and more important, we're talking serious problems with admissions that Joe wasn't admitting."

"We're talking public relations nightmare, too, especially with both the press and the police nosing around."

"I don't know if Babson knows about it and I'm afraid to be the one to tell him," Sally said.

I heard a banging noise and looked up. Rochester had gotten up from his place by the heater and was nosing his head against the bottom drawer of Joe's file cabinet, which Sally had left open.

"What's up, boy?" I asked, going over to him. "You have something else you want to point out to us?"

He shook his head and snorted. There were still a couple of thin manila folders left in the drawer, and I pulled them out. "What are these?" I asked.

"Joe's correspondence files. I haven't looked at them yet."

I opened the first folder and started flipping through pages. "Boring, boring, boring," I said. I went to the next, which was more of the same. Travel receipts, memos about various high schools and their college counselors. I didn't hit pay dirt until the last one."

It was a memo Joe had written to Babson, hand-typed on Eastern memo paper. In it, Joe announced his retirement from Eastern. He said he was using that opportunity to admit that he had been fabricating statistics.

"Wow," I said. "Something like that could destroy the campaign."

"Do you think anyone else knew about it?" Sally asked. "Maybe Babson did. Maybe he killed Joe to cover this up."

Like every expensive, private liberal arts college, Eastern had some serious problems-- declining applicant pool, less federal scholarship aid, rising tuition. And our problems were worse than we thought. "Babson's a little crazy," I said. "But murder? No. Plus he wouldn't have done anything to jeopardize the campaign."

I handed the memo to her. "Look, we've got to keep this a secret for a while. Let the campaign get rolling. We'll figure out how to let the news out little by little."

I went back to my office, got my coat and scarf, and took Rochester down the hill for a quick walk and so that we could grab lunch from one of the trucks. I ordered Rochester a plain hamburger, no bun. When I got back to my office I ate at my desk, feeding him bits of chopped beef between bites of my sandwich.

I went back to Blair Hall at two, taught the tech writing class about business letters, and worked at connecting their names to their faces. As usual in any class, a few kids stood out at first—Lou, the guy who was always working on papers, La'Rose, the black girl with the elaborate hairdos, Barbara, the tiny blonde elf. Once again, I thought Yenny was a girl and was confused when a boy answered as I called the roll. The other kids blended together but I hoped I'd get to know them all eventually.

From there, I walked over to the gym for a brainstorming session with Sam Boni. Athletic supporters (no pun intended) are among a college's most loyal and vocal fans. I was hoping that Sam would have some ideas about how we could reach out to them as part of the capital campaign. I found him up on a ladder in the new gym, peering above the acoustic ceiling tiles.

"So that's where you find your athletic talent," I said.

"No, this is where we find our leaky pipes. Under the job description for athletic director you find 'Responsible for maintenance of one new gym, poorly constructed, one old gym, seldom used, one aging field house and one poorly equipped boathouse, too far away to be practical.'"

The new gym wasn't all that new, but Eastern's original gym, a high-ceilinged square with wooden floors, was still used for occasional events. The new gym, built in the 1970s, had been state of the art when I was a student. "What's the matter with this gym?" I asked. "I always thought it was in terrific condition."

"You were also in school here twenty-five years ago."

I winced. "Don't remind me. But tell me what's wrong."

He counted off on his fingers. "Poor planning, shoddy construction, skimping on the quality of piping, inadequate ventilation. You want me to go on? I'd love to, but you're not supposed to speak ill of the dead. Our pal Joe awarded the contracts and supervised the construction of this place."

"Joe Dagorian?"

"One and the same. During that time when he was in charge of physical plant. Have you noticed we've already replaced that brick facing on the front of the building?"

"I just thought it was general beautification."

"Poor insulation. Water was seeping in through the mortar and cracking the walls. Hell of a job to fix it."

"You think he just did a bad job?" I asked.

"I think he let a lot of the contractors get away with murder. Either he didn't know what to look for, or he deliberately looked the other way."

"I can't believe Joe would do that to Eastern."

"I can believe anything of anybody,"Sam said. "Especially if there's money involved. I'm not saying anything, mind you. " He put his palms straight out in front of him. "But you get that idea when you live with these problems."

"And I always thought we had great facilities. How can we use this information to get donations to the capital campaign?"

"Come on into my office and I'll show you what I found." Sam was wearing a tight-fitting red alligator shirt, sweat pants and high-top sneakers. He still had an athlete's physique, the kind I had only aspired to when I was in college. Years of running had given me good cardiovascular conditioning and a certain flexibility, but I had never managed the kind of tone Sam had. It didn't seem fair that he was smart, too, but he had graduated cum laude from Pepperdine and had an MA in physical education and an MBA in management from USC. Word

101

around the campus had Sam aiming for a higher managerial role once the campaign was in full swing.

On the way we talked about the police progress on Joe's murder. "Sally said you two were looking for some information for the police. She said there were a lot of people who had grudges against Joe."

I looked at him. "You hear a lot from Sally"

He blushed a little. "We're trying to keep it quiet. Eastern's a small place and news travels fast."

"Your secret's safe with me."

When we got to his office, he pulled up a file on his computer and sent it to the printer. "This is a list of my priorities. We need a new weight room with some state-of-the-art equipment. I'd love to have a physical therapist on staff to work on conditioning with athletes across sports. I can always use more money for athletic scholarships. And we need funds for general maintenance on all facilities."

"From what I know from Mike, the general funds are the hardest to get," I said. "But I can help you put together some materials for the campaign to get specific donations—the weight room, the scholarships and so on. Can you put together a list of students I could interview and photograph? And do you have any good video clips from games? I'm thinking of doing more with YouTube and other social networking sites."

We made a list of everything we could do for each other, and I walked back to my office, thinking about Sally dating Sam. I had to admit to being jealous. I liked Sally and I had been thinking, way at the back of my mind, about asking her out, even though I was a lot older than she was.

I had thought once about dating Gail, the bakery owner, but she was a lot younger than I was, too. Was there something that kept me from looking at available women? Or was I just not running into them, working on a college campus?

Joe's House

I was depressed as I walked back up to Fields Hall through the cold, wet chill of February. Suddenly, Eastern College had become a hotbed of news, all bad. It was as if we had stripped the pleasant, small-town collegiate veneer off the place and found something ugly and sordid underneath.

When Horatio Wilcox, Eastern's founder, moved the college up the hill from its beginnings in a church in Leighville, he took over both the Fields estate and the Fields fortune. He hired a firm of architects to create a campus for his new school. The Collegiate Gothic style was flourishing in our vicinity at the University of Pennsylvania and Bryn Mawr College, and Wilcox wanted the same for his campus.

The major new buildings were Wilcox Hall, to house the liberal arts and humanities; Pennsylvania Hall, which held classrooms and laboratories for the physics, chemistry and mathematics departments; and President's Tower, a large granite bell tower. Dormitories and eventually fraternities followed, and then a new hall for the study of languages and the humanities in the 1940s. In the 1950s Eastern built a new laboratory building and then in the 1960s the new gym.

The campus, which had begun by dominating the top of the hill, as Fields had intended his mansion to do, began to spread over it. Long dormitories flanked the oval drive, fraternities and sororities sat on either side of the gates, and new construction spread over the back side of the hill. Only the main lawn, within the arc of the driveway, remained untouched. It was shaded by old elms and provided a pleasant place to relax or study on warm afternoons. An old wrought iron fence protected it from the clamor of Main Street, which stretched away east to the center of Leighville.

Rounding a corner, I saw Tony Rinaldi ahead of me and called to him.

103

"Just walking around," he said. "Sometimes I think that if I just spend enough time up here the answer will come to me."

"Well, it's a college. We're supposed to provide an education."

"And I wonder about that. What makes these kids come to Eastern, to Leighville? My father came to work in the Fields factory. I was born here, and there never seemed to be much reason to leave. But you came here to go to school. What made you do it?"

"Money," I said. "Eastern made me a better offer than any of the schools in the Ivy League. See, those schools all signed the Ivy Financial Agreement, which stipulates that no student should have to decide between any of the signors on the basis of financial aid. Eastern routinely makes a practice of over-guessing the Ivies and stealing away the middle-class ones who don't get a lot of financial aid elsewhere."

"Makes for a pretty middle-class school, doesn't it?"

"Oh, we give a lot of scholarships to smart kids from poor families, and a certain number of rich kids come here for the academics or because it's small. Our one disadvantage is our location. Leighville can't match the cosmopolitan atmosphere of Cambridge, New York or Princeton."

We walked along a path that had been cleared of slush, but a few little puddles remained. I walked carefully, but Rinaldi, in his shiny black boots, just plowed along. "So you came to Eastern in 1985," he said. "Why'd you leave?"

"I went to graduate school at Columbia, and then got a job in the city. Met my ex-wife, fell in love, got married. When she got the chance for a big job in California, we packed up and went. Never thought about coming back to Bucks County."

Tony already knew about my time in prison. "When I got out on parole, I didn't know where to go. But my father had just died and left me his townhouse, and it was easier to come back here than to start all over somewhere else."

We reached the front door of Fields Hall and Tony said, "Listen, Steve, I'm the first to admit it when I need some help. And right now my investigation is stalled. I cleared Norah Leedom and Thomas Taylor, and I can't find enough information on Bob Moran to get a subpoena. I spent the morning going through Mr. Dagorian's emails and phone records, and I didn't find anything I already knew."

"I found some things, though," I said. "Come on inside and I'll fill you in."

As we walked into my office, I told him about the problems Sam had found with the gym, and the statistics Joe had been fudging, and the resignation memo.

"You think President Babson knew about these inaccurate statistics? And the problems with the gym?"

"You'd think if he did, he'd have fired Joe on the spot," I said. "But Joe was still here."

"Could someone else have known about it, and be blackmailing Dagorian? This Zamboni guy?"

"Sam Boni, not Zamboni. Why kill Joe if the blackmailer could get money out of him?"

"Dagorian couldn't pay, or wouldn't," Tony said. "He was going to resign anyway. Maybe he threatened to take the blackmailer down with him." He sighed. "Every time I try to talk to somebody from this college I get stonewalled. It's the old town and gown thing. And it's not the first time it's happened to me lately. We got a tip that there were students up here selling steroids, but I haven't been able to dig any deeper than that."

For as long as the college had been in existence, there had been conflicts between it and the community. When I was in school at Eastern, Leighville residents complained when the college wanted to build a new gym on previously open land, and the college administration fought against passage of an ordinance that would restrict what it could do with its property. Students got into trouble at bars and stores, and sometimes thought they were better than the locals. Occasionally there had been violence, and the break-in rate soared during college vacations when students left valuables behind.

105

"What can I do to help?" I asked.

"I need more background on people who might have had a grudge against Joe Dagorian," he said. "It's my impression that this is an inside job, because of the circumstances. The killer had to be familiar with this building in order to know where Mr. Dagorian was going. He had to know about this event and that it would provide a good cover for him. We think he may have tried to hurt the college, too, by killing Mr. Dagorian at your party."

"You think someone killed Joe just to hurt Eastern?"

"He was killed because somebody wanted him dead. What I'd like you to do is just keep your ears and eyes open. Anything you hear, anything you see, that you think might be important, if you could let me know. I know a college is a little world of its own, and you being in this world you might catch something that an outsider wouldn't. You know, it's funny but even though I've lived here in Leighville all my life I've never been very comfortable up here at the college. And this murder doesn't make me feel any more comfortable. No, sir, not at all."

I looked at the clock and realized I was due in Blair Hall to teach the tech writing class. I hurried over there and played Perpetua Kaufman's video presentation on writing research papers. When the video was finished I asked, "Who has an idea about a topic?"

Dead silence.

"OK, let's talk about how to choose a topic. Let's say you're interested in the environment. That's a huge topic, so you have to narrow it down. Any ideas?"

"Global warming?" Lou suggested.

"Still a big topic. You could narrow it down to the shrinking of the polar ice cap, or rising sea levels, because big icebergs in the Arctic are melting."

"Or hurricanes," La'Rose said. "I read something how global warming leads to this El Nino thing, which makes more hurricanes."

"You could write about an endangered species," Barbara said. "Like an animal or a plant."

"Great. See how we're getting down to something that's manageable in a short paper? I want you all to spend some time brainstorming your topics, and then before the end of class we'll go over them again."

I sat down at my computer and answered emails, then walked around the room. Lou Segusi was working on a long paper about academic responsibility. "You've made a lot of progress," I said, looking over his shoulder.

"Oh, this is a paper for another class," he said. "I'm not sure what I'm going to write about here yet."

"Well, you should be focusing on this class while you're here. If you finish what you have to do for me, then you can do your other work."

"But this paper's due tomorrow," he said. "Please, prof?"

"You give me a topic, I'll let you keep going on that."

"How about that group Sister Perpetua belonged to?" he asked. "Bucks County Nature Conservancy? I was looking at their website and it looked really interesting. I could write about them."

The name was vaguely familiar but I couldn't place it. "What do they do?"

"Local activism for environmental stuff. They volunteer as docents at parks, and they do surveys of wildlife and stuff."

"Sounds good. That's an opportunity for primary research, too."

I walked back up to the front of the room. "Listen up for a minute," I said. "Lou's idea lends itself to primary research. You all know the difference between primary and secondary research?"

They looked like I'd asked for the difference between air and water. Something they should know, but couldn't quite put into words. "You do primary research when you go out and experience the world. You ask questions, look for things in the real world."

"Like the police?" La'Rose asked.

"Kind of," I thought, thinking of Tony Rinaldi and the way he was investigating Joe Dagorian's murder.

107

"You could write a questionnaire about attitudes toward smoking, or teenaged sex, or abortion, and then compile the results. Or in Lou's case, he could attend a meeting of the group he's interested in, maybe volunteer with them."

"And what's the other?" Barbara asked.

"Secondary research is the kind you guys usually do. You read books and magazine articles written about your subject, about the first-hand research other people have done."

They went back to work, and by the end of our hour and a quarter it looked like they were all on track to decent topics.

The rest of the afternoon passed quickly. I ran into Norah and Sally in the lobby of Fields Hall as we were all leaving for the day. "I have to go over to Joe's house and pick up some things," Norah said. "I'm not looking forward to it."

"Do you want us to come along with you?" Sally asked. "Steve and me?" Rochester barked once. "And Rochester, of course."

"That would be so nice," Norah said. "It'll be the first time I've been there since… well, you know."

Rochester hopped into the passenger seat of the BMW, and we followed Norah's SUV down the hill, with Sally behind us. We negotiated the suburban streets along the river to Joe's house. "You're going to have to be a good boy," I said to him. "No digging around in things that don't belong to you. You hear me?"

He just sat there with his head on his paws. Sometimes he's worse than a teenager.

The three of us parked on the street in front of Joe's house. "I just keep going over that evening in my mind," Norah said as we all walked up to the front door. "I keep feeling I might have seen something or heard something important but I just can't remember."

"Run through once again what you did that night," I suggested. "Sometimes it helps to have someone else listen."

Norah fished around in her shoulder bag for the key to Joe's front door, took a deep breath, and inserted it in the lock. The door swung open. The air inside was musty.

We walked inside, and she turned up the heat and started turning on lights. "I was talking with Mike MacCormac about John Babson-- we were watching him move around the room. I saw Babson head toward the French doors and I decided I'd go to outside myself and have a cigarette."

"So President Babson was outside, too?"

"I think so. I didn't see him out there. I was on the east side of the building, where Joe... was found."

"Did you see anyone else outside?"

Norah was quiet for a while. "I heard several of those young men from the Rising Sons. They were hiding outside behind the door that leads in to the admissions hallway, laughing and talking. I smelled some marijuana smoke. I found a sheltered place between trees and pulled out my cigarettes. Joe was pacing around outside like he had something serious on his mind. But when he saw me, he lit into me again about smoking."

"You shouldn't, you know," Sally said. "Sam shows his kids these slides of what their lungs look like after smoking. It's gruesome."

"I know, dear. I heard enough of it from Joe." She walked into the kitchen. There were dirty dishes in the sink and she began rinsing them and stacking them in the dishwasher. "I told him that he ought to stay out of my business," Norah continued. "He started yelling about selling the land in New Hampshire, and that's when I told him he frustrated me so much sometimes I could kill him."

"Which those women waiting to go inside overheard."

She nodded. "I stubbed out my cigarette and went inside. I didn't see Joe again until... until they took him away."

"So you didn't see Bob Moran? Apparently he saw you."

"The electric car man? What in the world was he doing there?"

"He's an Eastern alum. His son is applying for the fall class, and Joe wouldn't let him in."

"Really? Do you think he killed Joe?"

"Rinaldi says he doesn't have enough evidence to subpoena Moran's fingerprints," I said. "But he's looking into him."

Norah straighened up. "I need to find the deed for the land. Joe's interest becomes part of his estate and the attorney needs it. Will you be OK out here for a few minutes?"

"Sure," Sally said.

I walked over to Joe's bookcase and started browsing, while Sally sent someone—probably Sam Boni—a text message. As Norah had said once, Joe wasn't much for literature. Most of the books on the shelf were non-fiction, many of them about sports. I picked up a copy of *The Farmer's Almanac* and was paging through it when I realized Rochester was pawing at a pile of papers on the bottom shelf. They slid forward onto the ground. I said, "Oh, Rochester, what are you doing?"

He looked up at me with a doggy grin, like he was expecting a treat for messing up Joe's house. I sat down on the floor and started putting the papers back in order, Rochester's head in my lap, nosing at everything.

"This is getting old, Rochester," I said. "I wish you could talk, so you could just tell me what you want me to know."

He barked once.

"He agrees with you," Sally said, looking up from her phone. "You need a hand down there?"

"Sure. " The papers had slid everywhere. Most of them were copies of correspondence—it didn't look like Joe had much of a filing system. Insurance claims were next to newspaper clippings which were next to doctors' reports.

"This is weird," Sally said, holding up one piece of paper.

"Weird how?"

"This is a copy of a student's application essay and portfolio, from last year."

"Why would Joe have that at home?"

"That's a good question."

I looked over at it. The student was Barbara Seville, who was in my tech writing class, and it included a series of nature photographs she had taken.

"Put it aside," I said. "We can take it back to the college and see if it relates to anything."

Rochester kept nosing at the papers and I kept pushing him away. After a while, Norah came out of the bedroom with the paperwork she had come for, and she sat down on the floor with us and kept looking. "He was such a pack rat," she said. "Look at this. I remember when we went on this trip, a couple of years after we were married."

She held up the brochure for a small inn in Vermont. "Why in the world would he have kept this?"

"Maybe he had a good time," Sally said.

We ended up putting together a whole folder of questionable documents to look over ourselves and possibly pass on to Tony Rinaldi. We parted company then, and Rochester and I drove home.

A Gentleman and Verona

The next morning was bright and sunny, very unusual for February, and I relished my brief morning walk with Rochester. There was a slight wind that made the air crisp, but I zipped up my down parka, slipped on my rabbit fur-lined gloves, and strode off into the wind. Rochester, of course, had his own fur coat.

I was only moderately chilled by the time we got to Fields Hall, and it took just a cup of hot chocolate and the warmth of my office to put me right again. Looking over the list of Sam's priorities for the athletic program, I remembered what he had said about Joe's supervision of the gym construction.

He was obviously not qualified to manage a project like that, but because he was a loyal Eastern man he accepted his assignment and muddled through. Joe's main skill seemed to be his love of Eastern College and his loyalty to it. I wondered if that was what had also gotten him killed. It struck me as funny that Joe would have made a great fund-raiser for Eastern if he hadn't been so opposed to the idea.

More worrying than Joe's botched construction job was his inability to handle the admissions office. He was good at convincing kids to come to Eastern, one on one. But the fudged numbers that Sally was discovering were dangerous. Suppose that information got out to the press and the general public? Eastern's reputation would take a nose dive, and the capital campaign would flounder. People are much more willing to give their money to a successful, thriving college than one that's down on its luck.

Even more worrying was the realization that Joe might have been killed to prevent that information getting out. Suppose he was going to retire, as he had hinted to Norah, and he wanted to leave with a clean slate. And suppose his malice toward fund-raising led him to see an opportunity to wipe us out while coming clean on his own. I could see someone stopping him, and unfortunately the someone I kept seeing was John

112

William Babson. I'd have to mention to Tony Rinaldi that Norah had seen Babson heading outside just before Joe was murdered.

Long before the launch party and Joe's murder, I had scheduled a trip to New York to meet with press contacts and alumni and pitch stories about the college. I was tempted to cancel, but I thought it would be better to present my agenda than let the press run away with their own take on Joe's death. I spent most of Thursday confirming my appointments for the next day and putting together the materials I wanted to take with me.

Just before five, I started to pack my briefcase with Eastern catalogs and press kits. I had just run out of room and started to put the overflow into a pair of plastic shopping bags when Sally came in with the file on Verona Santander, the girl who had complained about Ike Arumba's behavior, and a copy of Joe's letter about Ike.

"I'd hate to have to push this forward," Sally said. "But if the girl has a real complaint then I need to do something about it."

"Ike's graduating this term, isn't he? What could happen to him?"

"Hard to say without knowing exactly what he did. He could be suspended or even expelled. I know he's looking for a job in college admissions after he graduates, and if he gets something like this on his record I can't imagine any college that would hire him."

"That's tough. You think it could be a motive for murder?"

"Ike? You think maybe he killed Joe?"

"Norah said that she saw Ike and some of the guys from the Rising Sons outside getting high just before Joe was killed. That gives Ike opportunity. And now he's got a motive, and he could easily have picked up a knife from the buffet line."

Sally shook her head. "He seems like such a nice guy, though."

"But drugs can change you," I said. "Maybe Ike started getting paranoid about Joe, and the dope made it worse."

113

Sally helped me carry my promotional material out to the BMW, Rochester frolicking around us. "Are you taking Rochester with you?" she asked, as she leaned down to pet him.

"Are you kidding? I can only imagine the damage this mutt could do in a Manhattan hotel room. He's staying with my friend Rick."

Rochester must have recognized Rick's name, because he barked and nodded his head.

We drove home, and I walked and fed Rochester, then packed my suitcase, including a rolling duffel full of Eastern flyers and merchandise. We'd had pens made up for the launch party, and I also had some no-slide doohickeys you put on the back of cell phones, with the Eastern logo, and some other giveaways.

Just after seven, I loaded it all in the car along with Rochester's bowl, a canvas bag of his toys, and the remains of a 20-pound bag of dog chow. "Come on, boy," I said, waving his leash. "Let's go for a ride."

He scrambled behind the dining room table and put his head behind one of the table legs. "Rochester," I said. "No nonsense. I have a train to catch."

I had to get down on my hands and knees and hook the leash onto his collar, then pull. He resisted for a while, his claws scrabbling on the tile floor, but eventually I got him out from under the table. Then, of course, it all became a big game to him. He jumped up on me and stuck his nose in my crotch.

I scratched behind his ears, then he got down and rushed toward the front door. "Wacky dog," I said.

We drove over to Rick's house, near the Delaware in the oldest part of town. It had been his parents' place, and he had bought it from them when they moved to Florida. I opened the gate to his fenced-in front yard and let Rochester loose, then returned to the car for all the doggy stuff. By the time I had it in hand Rick had the front door open, and Rascal had rushed out to romp with my dog.

"You didn't need to bring all this stuff," Rick said. "I've got dog chow, and toys, and a bowl."

"Rochester likes his own stuff."

"Rochester's a spoiled brat." Rick reached down to scratch behind the golden retriever's ears. "Aren't you? Are you the most spoiled dog in Stewart's Crossing?"

Rascal came blasting across the yard to get his share of the attention. "I think he's got some competition for that title," I said.

I squatted down to hug Rochester one last time. "You behave for Uncle Rick, and play nice with Rascal." He woofed and nodded his head.

He tried to follow me out the front gate to the car, and when I closed him inside the yard he sat on his haunches and looked at me. He barked twice, and I said, "I'm coming back, dog. Don't get your nuts in a twist."

I got in the car, and even over the engine I could hear him howling mournfully. Rick just laughed as I drove away. I parked the BMW at the train station in Trenton and caught a late evening train to New York. It was nearly eleven by the time I was checked into my room, in a very old and not very elegant hotel on the Upper West Side. I thought briefly of Rochester, wondering if Rick was giving him his late-night walk, and then I was asleep.

The next morning I retrieved coffee and donuts from a café around the corner and returned to my room, where I set up my agenda for the day. Before I left, I called Barnard College information and got Verona Santander's phone number. When I reached her at her dorm, she wasn't eager to talk to me. "It's important, Verona." I explained about Joe's murder and Sally's problems in organizing the office. "It would help us to understand. To know what's what."

"Well, OK," she said. "But you'll have to come up here. I have a class from 3 until 5. Can you meet me at a coffee shop called Papa's on Amsterdam at 118th at a quarter past five?"

I checked my watch. "I've got an appointment at four myself. I can shoot up on the subway after that."

My first appointment was with a newsmagazine writer who'd gone to Eastern. His office was a cubicle high up in a skyscraper but stuck in the middle of a warren of similar cubicles.

"Thanks for thinking of me, Steve. I'm always interested in news of my alma mater. You've been getting a lot of press lately."

"Not exactly the kind we'd like." I settled back in the easy chair across from his desk. The walls of the cubicle were about six feet high and covered with articles, posters and ads, mostly clipped out of his magazine. "We want to develop a particular image for Eastern. You can understand that-- we want everyone to know the Eastern that you and I do."

He nodded. "I'm impressed with your fund-raising campaign. Five hundred million is a lot of money for a small school like Eastern to raise. I hope you don't expect to get much of it from me. " He laughed.

"The money people come after me," I said, and we both laughed. "What we want right now is your good will. We want you to think of Eastern when you need a comment from an academic source." I dug into my briefcase. "I've brought you some of our recent materials. I don't expect you to make us a cover story, but I do hope that when you call Harvard or Yale for a comment on computer education or financial aid or athletic recruiting, you'll think of Eastern too. We're representative of the kind of things that are happening to small private colleges around the country, and some of our professors are doing headline research. Here's our experts list-- if you need an academic comment for a story on anything from the drought in Africa to unemployment in Detroit, we've got a faculty member with something to say."

It had been hard work to get professors at Eastern to relate their research to contemporary topics. It seemed they never studied concrete things like consumer purchasing, but instead looked at "The purchase of small consumer goods in Henry James' *The Golden Bough*." Purely academic research. If we'd had a business school or a medical school my job would have been easier, but we had a few sociologists and historians who ought to make it into an article somewhere down

116

the road. We chatted for a while about Eastern and I went on to other interviews.

Around 4:45 I caught the subway uptown to Morningside Heights. Rush hour had already begun and the trains were jammed with people in heavy winter coats carrying shopping bags and briefcases. Almost every woman seemed to be wearing a navy or gray pinstriped business suit with a white blouse tied into a bow, carrying a leather folder, and wearing running shoes with brightly colored swirls and logos on them.

I got to the coffee shop first, and I sat at a booth in the back with a view of the door. Verona came in a few minutes later. She was about five foot six, very pretty, with frizzy brown hair pulled into a knot and tied to the side with a pink scarf. She was wearing a knee-length gray down coat with a thick pink vertical stripe, and I looked up and smiled when she looked at me.

She came back to the booth. "Mr. Levitan?"

I stood up and stuck out my hand. "You must be Verona. Thanks for agreeing to meet me."

When she hung up her coat, I saw she was wearing blue jeans and a pink sweatshirt that said, "Go Climb A Rock" underneath it. The waiter came by and she ordered a Tab. "I'll have coffee," I said. "Very light, with sugar."

"How can I help you?" she asked.

"As I told you, Eastern's director of admissions was murdered recently. His assistant, Sally Marston, is a friend of mine, and when we were going through his files to find out where things stand, she found a cryptic reference to you."

"To me?"

I nodded. "One of Sally's best assistants is a student named Ike Arumba." Verona grimaced when she heard the name. "Apparently Joe Dagorian had some problem with Ike, and it relates to a letter you sent. We can't find the letter in the files, but we did find a draft of a letter recommending that Ike be expelled from Eastern because of something involving you. I'd like to find out what you said in your letter that turned Joe against Ike."

Our drinks came, and Verona took a long sip of her Tab. "Two of my really good friends went to Eastern the year before I graduated from high school," she said. "They both liked the school a lot, so I went out to visit them in the early fall and I really liked the campus, too. I filled out my application in December and sent it in, and in January Eastern had a reception in Portland-- that's where my folks live. Since they were away on vacation then, I went to the reception by myself. Ike Arumba gave a presentation on Eastern. I was really into going there then."

"What made you change your mind?"

She didn't say anything. "I promise you I won't repeat this unless it's necessary, and I'll get your permission before we involve you any further."

She nodded. "Afterwards I went up to tell him how much I enjoyed the presentation and that I was really looking forward to going to Eastern. See, my grades were good but I didn't do real well on the SATs and I thought if I was nice to him he'd help me get in."

She looked to me for reassurance. "It's easier for the admissions staff when they can attach a face or a personality to the application," I said.

"He was really nice and he asked me if I wanted to have dinner with him. He said he was all alone in town and didn't know anybody, and I thought he was kind of cute."

"And?"

"Well, we went to this restaurant, and we had a couple of drinks and then dinner and then a couple more drinks and then he asked me to go to bed with him."

"Good god!" I said. "What an asshole!"

"You've got it," she said. "I did think he was cute, and I really wanted to go to Eastern. And I was pretty naive and I thought, like, maybe if I don't he'll fix it so I won't get in. So we went over to his hotel room and, well, you know."

"It's absolutely the most unprofessional thing I ever heard," I said. "But just to be clear, you did have sex with him?"

"Yes. He was bummed that I wasn't a virgin, but afterwards he gave me cab fare to get back to my car, and then a few weeks later I got into Eastern."

"And then you wrote the letter?"

She shook her head. "I decided that Eastern had to be really sleazoid to send a jerk like him off to recruit, and like, did I really want to go to college with sleazebags? So I decided to go to Barnard, and then I sort of forgot about it. But I'm, like, really involved with the women's center at Barnard, and when I talked about it everybody said I should write a letter to Mr. Dagorian and tell him what happened. I did that about a month ago, and he called me up and we talked about it, and he said he would see that Ike got disciplined. That's the last I heard."

I paid the check and we walked out together. "I appreciate your telling me this, Verona. I know it doesn't help much, but please accept my apologies for what happened. I went to Eastern myself and I know that creeps like Ike don't come through very often."

"Thanks. Anyway, I really like Barnard and I'm glad I didn't go to Eastern. I mean, god, to be out in the boondocks like that! After all, I came east to get to civilization, after Portland and all."

As the subway rattled and clanked downtown, I wondered if Joe's threat would have been enough to motivate Ike to murder. Joe could not only destroy Ike's chance for an Eastern diploma, forcing him to leave without a degree, but he could derail Ike's plans for a career in college admissions.

I had made a mistake myself, so perhaps I was more sympathetic to Ike than Joe would have been. As well, I recognized that we only had Verona's word for what happened. Suppose she had seduced Ike? Or what if she was just nuts, and had made the whole thing up? Both were possible.

When Mary suffered her first miscarriage, she had gone on a spending spree, plunging us deep into credit card debt. It had taken us two years of overtime and freelance work to climb back out of that morass. Then

119

she got pregnant again, and we both felt like we were on top of the world—debt free, ready to start our family.

Then she miscarried again. I was so frightened she'd fall into the same pattern again that I hacking into the main credit card databases and put alerts on all her cards. A couple of days later, the police came for a visit, and my downward slide began.

So I understood how scary consequences could be. But did Ike? And had he done something to protect himself?

No Satisfaction

I met my graduate school roommate, Tor, for dinner that night, at a steakhouse in midtown. He was a Swedish exchange student in business school, and for a few years we were young and single together in the city. He was a successful investment banker, married to a former model, with two kids in expensive private schools.

Every time we met I couldn't help considering the different directions our lives had taken. Tor was generous to a fault; it would never have occurred to him to criticize me for my choices or make me feel bad about the difference in our fortunes. He was a couple of inches taller than I was, with blond hair so light it was almost white. I couldn't remember if he had looked different when we were in our twenties, though I was sure he'd looked a lot less prosperous.

"So you've joined the ranks of the gainfully employed," Tor said as we sat down. He still had a touch of his Swedish accent, which came through in the unaccustomed emphasis on certain syllables. "And how is it, this new job?"

"A little creepy." I told him about Joe's murder.

"Not another one. I don't know that I want to keep hanging around with you. People you know end up dead."

"People die all the time," I said, as the waiter approached. Tor ordered us both some very expensive Scotch. Without even looking at the menu he said, "I'll have the 24-ounce Porterhouse. Baked potato with butter, and creamed spinach. Caesar salad."

"Make it two of everything," I said.

When the waiter left Tor said, "Yes, people die. But around you they get murdered." He looked at me. "You're not snooping around in this murder, are you?"

I shifted uncomfortably in my seat. "I know the detective, from when my neighbor was murdered. He's been asking me for information."

"Remember what happened to you last time, Steve," he said. "And to Rochester. You don't want that again."

"I'm staying out of trouble. Scout's honor." I held up two fingers.

"Bjorn is in the Boy Scouts," Tor said. "So I know that you are supposed to hold up three fingers, not two."

"Whatever. How are Bjorn and Lucia, and Sandra?"

Tor had married Sandra, a former fashion model, a year after I left for the West Coast with Mary. Bjorn, ten, and Lucia, eight, were named after Tor's parents, still living in Stockholm.

"All fine. Bjorn is too smart. He already has an argument for everything. He is reading Dickens now. Do you believe that? And Lucia is studying ballet. She is already the best in her class."

I couldn't help being jealous. Tor was one of my best friends, and I was happy about every good thing that had happened to him, from his business success to his loving marriage to his healthy, happy children. But whenever I saw him, I started comparing his life to mine.

The waiter brought the salads, and we went on to talk about a lot of different things, catching up in bits and pieces on our lives. "You ever hear from Mary?" he asked, as we dug into the porterhouse.

"Not since last year. I think it's best. She has a new husband, a new baby. And I have Rochester."

"Yes, Rochester. You keep sending me pictures of your dog, which is causing a lot of trouble in my household."

"How so?"

"Bjorn and Lucia want a dog. 'Uncle Steve has Rochester. Why can't we have a dog?'" He speared a chunk of beef. "I tell them that Uncle Steve lives in the country with lots of space for a dog to run. We live in the city."

"And does that work?"

"No. The family next door bought a bichon frise last month. My children are over the moon. " He ate the

122

meat on his fork, and then sighed. "Maybe you can recommend a breeder? We could drive out to Stewart's Crossing when the weather warms up, visit you and look for a dog."

"I'll look around."

"Good. I will put the burden on you. Don't be surprised if you begin getting very demanding emails from my children, though."

As usual, Tor insisted on paying for dinner. We hugged outside the restaurant, where a Lincoln Town Car was waiting to speed him back to his family. "I can drop you somewhere?" he asked.

"I'll walk. It was good to see you, Tor. I can't wait to see Sandra and the kids out in the country in the spring."

I walked back to my hotel, hands in my pockets, full of a good dinner and excellent Scotch, yet still unsatisfied.

Though the next morning was Saturday, I had been able to set up a heavy round of appointments. I started with an editor at another newsmagazine, where I repeated the message I had given out the day before, only this time in a corner office with wraparound windows and a magnificent view of midtown and lower Manhattan. You could tell the guy had read all those "power" books-- navy suit, silk tie, expensive Italian leather shoes. His desk was enormous and completely empty, except for a small pile of papers next to his right hand, a telephone with intercom and speaker, and a small, silver-framed photo of his wife and children.

My chair was a little too low, so I had to look up to him and struggle to maintain my posture. I passed on the same materials, and emphasized the experts list again. At the end of our meeting he escorted me to the elevator, which was supposed to show what a valued visitor I was.

I had lunch at a private club downtown with a friend who was a reporter on the *Wall Street Journal*. The dining room was small and once again the views panoramic, this time of New York harbor.

I talked about Eastern for a while, until the food arrived. "I'm surprised you're out talking to reporters," my friend said, as he speared a forkful of chicken. "With all the trouble at Eastern."

"Joe Dagorian's death is a tragedy," I said. "But there's so much else going on—so many good things. That's what I'm here to talk about."

"I'm hearing about more than just Dagorian's death. What about all the security problems?"

"Any college is going to have issues. Even one in a pastoral setting like Eastern's. You can't get away from the real world, even in a place like this." I motioned to the elegant room around us, filled with the demure clink of glasses and the gentle rustle of cloth napkins.

I speared a couple of the baby carrots and zucchini that artfully decorated the plate. "I'll admit, we have had some problems with dorm break-ins, and the homeless in Leighville get up to the campus sometimes. But we're working on fixing those problems."

"And have the police caught whoever killed Dagorian?"

"As far as I know, it's still an open investigation. But that's police business."

He didn't appear to be completely satisfied, but I did manage to shift the conversation to the need for new science labs to keep up with the constant changes in technology and research, and he admitted he'd been working on an article on that very subject, and might be able to work Eastern into it.

It was late afternoon by then. I could have packed up and driven back to Leighville, but I knew Rochester was fine with Rick, and frankly, I wanted to spend some more time in the city. I love Stewart's Crossing, and working at Eastern, but I also get energized from spending time in New York.

I took the subway up to Times Square and walked down to the TKTS booth, where I joined the end of a long line. I was shifting from foot to foot, trying to stay warm, as the line snaked around, doubling back on itself, when I spotted her.

124

It was the hair, first. Masses of reddish-brown hair, tumbling over her shoulders, barely kept under control by a couple of hairpins in the shape of butterflies. But it wasn't until she turned around and our eyes met that I was sure.

"Dr. Weinstock?" I asked. "I'm Steve Levitan from the alumni office at Eastern."

"We met at the fund-raiser," she said. "Please, call me Lili. When I'm away from the college I'm always afraid that if someone hears me called "Dr. Weinstock" I'll be expected to perform CPR or deliver a baby."

"What are you seeing?" I asked.

"Depends on what's available by the time I get up to the booth. Something fun, something musical. I wish more people in daily life would break out into song."

"I'm hoping to get a ticket for the revival of South Pacific," I said. "I want to hear Bloody Mary sing *Bali Hai* and pretend I'm living on a tropical island instead of Bucks County in the winter."

"I could go for that," she said.

I lifted up the chain between the two lines. "Why don't you join me?"

"Sounds like a plan. " Only then did I notice she was wearing high heels—but she managed to duck beneath the chain with grace.

"What brings you into the city?" I asked.

"Photography exhibit at the Museum of Modern Art."

"Really? You like photography? So do I. I've started taking lots of digital pictures of my dog lately."

"It's my specialty," she said. "I have a few photos in the current exhibition and I gave a presentation this afternoon."

Oops. She wasn't some amateur photo buff. "Oh. Wow."

"You use your cell phone?" she asked as we inched forward.

I pulled it from my pocket. "You need to make a call?"

"No, dummy. Do you use the phone to take pictures of your dog?"

"Oh. Yeah."

"Well. Show me."

"Oh, no. They're just amateur shots."

She looked down over the rims of her red glasses. I could imagine her looking just that way at her students.

"He is very photogenic," I admitted. I clicked to the photo app and pulled up the folder of pictures of Rochester.

She took the phone from me and began looking through the shots. "Good composition," she said. "You have a good eye for movement, too. " She pointed at a picture of Rochester leaping through the air about to catch a Frisbee Rick had tossed for him. "What's his name?"

"Him? He's just an old high school friend. Rick. We're both divorced, and he just got a dog of his own."

"Not the guy. The dog."

Something about Lili Weinstock kept knocking me sideways, so I couldn't concentrate. "Oh. Rochester."

"After the city?"

"No, from *Jane Eyre*. He used to belong to my next-door neighbor, and she gave him his name."

"I love goldens," she said, as we rounded the corner, and the ticket window was within sight. "I've been thinking of getting a dog, now that I can finally settle down. Maybe next year I can move out of my apartment, buy a house. Then I might actually feel like I belong somewhere."

"You don't feel like you belong in Leighville yet?"

She shook her head. "Especially not with all the security issues that have been popping up. My students are often working in studio very late, and I worry about them getting back to their dorms safely."

"Have you heard of any issues?" I asked. "Because I haven't. I think the papers are manufacturing problems just to keep Joe's death on the front page."

"It's my responsibilty to look after my students," she said. "I'm thinking of shutting down the studios at ten. I already tell them to call security for a ride back to the dorms, even the boys. You can't be too careful."

It never seemed to stop, I thought, as we inched forward. Joe's death was a tragedy, for sure, but the

126

fact that it kept reverberating around the college was even worse.

The wrangler called us up to the ticket window. "I'll get the tickets if you agree to have dinner with me," I said. "That is, if you don't have any other plans?"

"I'd be delighted to have dinner with you," she said.

It was too early to eat by the time we had our tickets. "I need to stop by my hotel," Lili said. "Suppose we meet at Donatello's on West 45th at six o'clock?"

"Sounds like a plan," I said.

She took one of my hands in her two gloved ones. "I'm glad I ran into you, Steve. See you at six."

She smiled, then turned and walked away. "Yes, see you then," I called.

I resisted the urge to skip down the street. I had a date! With a gorgeous woman! Who liked golden retrievers!

I called Rick when I got back to my room. "How's Rochester?" I asked.

"You should see him boss Rascal around. It's amazing. If you can stay in New York an extra couple of days he might have Rascal fully trained."

"Who knows? I've got a hot date tonight."

"What, you've finally figured out there no decent women in Bucks County? You pick this one up in Times Square?"

"I did. At the TKTS booth. And actually she lives in Leighville, and teaches at Eastern."

"See, I'd never think to go to New York to pick up local women. Maybe that's my problem."

"You've got bigger problems than that," I said. "Take care of Rochester. I'll call you when I get back to town tomorrow."

The Taste of Lipstick

I felt as nervous as a teenager as I walked down West 45th Street that evening. The sidewalk bustled with pedestrians in winter coats, prosperous-looking couples, slouching teenagers, and working people heading homeward. I couldn't remember the last time I'd had a date.

I met Mary at a party in New York, and we'd had the same kind of initial connection I had with Lili. We spent hours talking to each other that night and kept on seeing each other until we moved in together. I didn't consider that meeting a date—and I couldn't conjure up a memory of any girl before her.

A stiff wind swept down the street and I shivered. Then I saw Lili approaching, wearing the same oversized wool trench coat she'd been wearing in the TKTS line, and I couldn't help grinning like an idiot.

We checked our coats just inside the restaurant door. Lili was wearing a tight-waisted red blouse that matched her eyeglasses, and a swirling, knee-length skirt in a floral print. I had ditched my suit, but all I'd brought with me beyond it was a pair of LL Bean jeans and a light blue long-sleeve polo shirt. I felt underdressed.

"You look lovely," I said, holding the chair for her. "I'm afraid I didn't bring any date clothes with me."

"When you've traveled as much as I have you tend to be prepared for any eventuality," she said. "Even a date with a handsome man."

Something warm bubbled up from the bottom of my stomach. "I'd like a kir," please," she told the waiter.

"Make it two," I said. "I used to work for a boss years ago who insisted that you should order an aperitif before a fine meal rather than dulling your palate with scotch or whiskey."

"Is this going to be a fine meal?"

"I don't see how it couldn't be, with you across the table from me."

"You're smooth, Steve," she said.

The waiter brought our cocktails and we toasted each other, then looked down at the menu. "Tortellini alla panna," I said, pointing. "My favorite."

"No!" she said. "I always order tortellini. The first time I ever had it was at this little restaurant along the Brenta river, between Padua and Venice. The people I was with insisted I order the tortellini in brodo, and I just fell in love."

"My story isn't so romantic," I said. "I used to live in the city and my ex-wife and I went to a lot of Italian restaurants. She hated to order the same thing over and over again and she made me try a lot of different dishes."

"Ex-wife?" she asked.

I nodded. "Married for twelve years. Divorced two years ago. How about you?"

"Married an Italian I met on my junior year abroad," she said. "I dropped out of college after that term and moved to Milan with him. I got a job as an assistant to a fashion photographer and fell in love with photography. Two years later I was divorced, back in college and finishing my BFA."

The waiter returned with a platter of foccacia, a bottle of olive oil, and a black pepper grinder. We both ordered the tortellini and dipped crusts of bread into the peppered oil.

"Wow, this is great," I said.

"I learned a lot about Italian food during those two years," she said. "The chef here, Donatello Nobatti, is amazing, and whenever I come to New York I eat here."

"So," I said. "BFA?"

She nodded. "Then an MFA in photography. Worked as a photographer myself, married an editor for a fashion magazine. He had a great eye for models—unfortunately, more than his eye got involved. Divorced him, then started teaching. Got a couple of one-year visiting artist gigs, then this opportunity opened up and I came to Leighville."

She dipped another piece of bread in the oil. "How about you?"

"Grew up in Stewart's Crossing, just down the river from Leighville. Went to Eastern. MA in English from Columbia, met my ex, got married, moved with her to Silicon Valley so she could immerse herself in her career."

"Hence the divorce," Lili said.

It would have been easy to agree and move the conversation on. But I had the feeling Lili was the kind of woman who liked cards on the table.

"That was certainly part of it. I was working as a technical writer for a computer company, and I got into hacking. Mary had a miscarriage, and things were tough between us. She went on a shopping spree that put us in the hole for a year. Then she got pregnant again and we were both so happy."

I paused to sip my kir. "She lost that baby, too, and I was scared she'd run up our credit cards again, so I hacked the credit bureaus and flagged her cards."

"You can do that?"

"I could. And I did. And I got caught, and I went to prison. While I was serving my time, my father died, and Mary divorced me. When I came out I moved back to Stewart's Crossing to lick my wounds and start over again."

I smiled. "And that's my story. Tell me about the pictures you have in the museum exhibit. What do you photograph?"

We talked about photography, and New York, and a bunch of other things I couldn't remember even an hour later. She had very kissable lips, highlighted with red lipstick, and in between thinking about how beautiful she was and how intriguing, I wondered what it would be like to kiss her.

Somehow we finished dinner and walked to the theater, where we sat close together and mouthed the words to the songs along with the cast. By the end of the show I was intoxicated with romance and passion and music. We began filing out of the theater and got stuck in a bottleneck a few feet from the single exit door. I could no longer resist—I turned and kissed Lili on the lips, very lightly and quickly.

I'd forgotten what lipstick tasted like. It had been a long time since I'd kissed anyone on the lips, but the feelings came spiraling back.

When I backed away I looked at Lili's eyes. They sparkled in the theater's lights. She took my hand in hers and squeezed, and we shuffled forward, holding hands.

"A nightcap?" I asked when we reached the street.

"I wish I could," she said. "But I have a command performance tomorrow morning at the Brooklyn Museum, and I need to get to bed, and then do some preparation in the morning."

I nodded. "I'd like to see you again in Leighville."

"Count on it. " She leaned forward, and we kissed again, up against the wall of the theater, out of the way of the hurrying crowds. Her lips were cold against mine, but they warmed up. I resisted the urge to pull her too close, just savoring the way the chilly air heightened the floral smell of her perfume, the way strands of her hair brushed against my face.

Then she backed away. "I see a cab," she said. "Ciao, cara!" She stepped toward the street and flagged down the cab. As she stepped into it, she blew me a kiss, and I mimed catching it in my hand and pressing my fingers to my lips. " My last vision was of her laughing as the cab drove away.

20 – 99% Perspiration

I left my suitcase with the valet at the hotel and walked up to H & H Bagels, where I bought a dozen in assorted varieties to take back to Stewart's Crossing with me. I had a salt bagel with a shmear and a Doctor Brown's black cherry soda, then retrieved my suitcase and took the train back to Trenton.

Rochester was romping in Rick's yard with Rascal when I pulled up. As soon as he saw the BMW he lit across the yard, slamming into the fence. "Hold on, hold on," I said, scrambling out of the car. I reached over the fence to pet his head as Rick came out of the front door.

"You sure you can't leave him here for a couple of days?" he asked. "Rascal hasn't chewed anything in the house since Rochester got here."

"Not a chance. This boy is coming home with me. " Rochester woofed and shook his head.

Driving back home, with Rochester on the seat next to me, I thought about Liliana Weinstock. Should I call her? Text her? Post something on her Facebook page that said, "Thanks for the great kiss?"

I felt like a teenager again, and I wasn't sure that was a good thing, at forty-three. I settled for sending her an email, from my college address to hers, saying that it was great to run into her in New York, and I hoped we'd get together again now that we were both back in Bucks County.

I spent some of the afternoon at the kitchen table, writing up my meetings, sending email thank yous and making plans to follow up with the reporters. Rochester sat at his customary post on the stair landing, two paws hanging over the tread, supervising. I couldn't help checking my email every hour or so, nervous about what kind of response I might get from Lili.

I knew she had that presentation to give at the Brooklyn Museum, and that she might not even return to Bucks County until late in the day. And there was no guarantee she'd even check her college email until the next day.

I admit to checking her faculty web page, which had a very flattering picture of her that reminded me of our kiss. And I might even have done some Googling, finding records of her past exhibitions and seeing some very beautiful photos she had taken. All in the name of research, of course. But by the time I turned off the computer and took Rochester for his before-bed walk, I had still received no response from her.

Monday morning, I woke before Rochester. He lying next to my bed, snoring lightly and probably dreaming about his wild weekend with Rick and Rascal. It gave me no small pleasure to nudge him awake. He yawned, but stayed flat on the floor. "Huh, don't like it when the shoe's on the other paw, do you?" I said. I toed him in the side again. "Come on, get up, you lazy lump."

Wrong move. He sprung up and began dancing around me in circles. I guess Rascal didn't wear him out enough. Outside, he was all business, striding forward on all four legs, barely stopping to sniff before peeing, pooping his guts out, then tugging me back home.

Security had been tightened on the campus as a result of all the newspaper articles. The guards at the front gate were taking their jobs more seriously, too, and the back and side gates into the campus were now either closed or manned by guards. I had to show my ID to get into the parking lot, and again at the front door of Fields Hall.

Once in my office, I wrote a report on my trip, and a series of thank-you notes to the people I had met. Dezhanne came in for a while to answer the phone and I read through the Sunday papers. The Leighville *Gazette* featured an in-depth look at security problems at Eastern College, which highlighted the fact that a ruthless killer was still on the loose.

Babson called at ten to rant about the poor press we were getting. I almost told him it wasn't my fault Joe got killed, or that the police couldn't seem to latch onto the guy who did it. But I knew that it was a touchy subject with him so I held back.

Four newspapers and the AP wire called to see if there had been any new developments in the case, and I told them no. Babson declined an opportunity to be interviewed on the campus radio station about security problems, and a TV station in Philadelphia called to say they might be interested in sending a camera crew up, if there were any new developments in the case. I said I would let them know.

I left Rochester snoozing in my office and met Sally for lunch at the Cafette, an on-campus sandwich shop in an old carriage house behind Fields Hall. It was a worn, homey-looking place, with old wooden picnic tables and benches. We snared one of the few single tables, off in the corner next to the remains of a brick chimney. Sally was eager to hear about my meeting with Verona Santander.

"She seemed like a real nice, well-adjusted girl," I said. "Not the kind who'd make up stories or hold a grudge. Your basic college freshman."

"What did she say about Ike?"

"Well, it's kind of hard to believe, but like I say, she doesn't seem to have much reason to lie."

I told Sally Verona's story, and afterwards she sat back in her seat and said, "Shit. What an awful thing to do. And when he seemed like such a good kid."

"Even good kids have their faults," I said. "His is just a little worse than most."

"Not just a little. A lot. I mean, that's a serious breach of ethics. To promise a girl admission if she sleeps with you. " She shook her head.

"She never said he promised."

"Even so, just to make the proposition is a serious breach," Sally said. "Why the hell did this have to happen now? When I'm so swamped and I have a million other problems?"

"What are you going to do about it?"

"I don't know. Ike is graduating this semester and I don't think it's fair to expel him when we have so little evidence. It happened a year ago, no one was hurt, and it's going to be Ike's word against this girl's. I'm going to have to let him go. I'll just make up an excuse. I can't take the risk that he'll compromise the office again."

134

"You aren't going to confront him with Verona's story?"

"He'll probably deny it and we'll have a scene. No, I'll just tell him there was an indication in Joe's files that he was to be let go, and I have to go along with Joe's plans, even though I don't understand them."

I did some more work back at the office, and after making sure Dezhanne had showed up to man the phones while I was gone, I went to teach the tech writing class. We talked some more about research, and how to structure a research paper. Then I set them loose to look for information on their research topics.

As I walked around the room, I noticed that once again Lou Segusi seemed to be busy working on a paper for some other class. I wondered how many papers the kid had to write in one term.

"I tried to contact that group," he said, popping up an internet browser that hid the document he was working on. "See? The Bucks County Nature Conservancy. But both the phone numbers have been disconnected."

He pointed at the bottom of the screen. "That first number, that's Sister Perpetua's. I cross-referenced it with the Yahoo people search."

I recognized the Stewart's Crossing exchange. "And the other?"

"Belongs to some guy named Joe. It's shut off, too. " He quickly copied the number, then pasted it into the search box. "Dagorian, Joseph R. " came up as the result.

"Joe Dagorian?" I asked.

"Yeah, that's the guy. You know him?"

"I did. He was in charge of admissions here. He was murdered a couple of weeks ago."

"No!" La'Rose said. "I read about that. Mr. Dagorian was really nice. He recruited me to come to Eastern."

I moved on down the line of computers, and Lou went back to whatever he was working on. It was a pretty big coincidence that both Joe and Perpetua had worked for the Nature Conservancy, and both were dead.

But was it? Both of them worked at Eastern, too. Joe had been around the college forever; he might have known Perpetua, and known she was interested in ecological subjects. And besides, Perpetua's death was an accident, wasn't it?

After class, I walked outside with Lou Segusi and Barbara Seville. As we got outside she suddenly took off, runing up to a big black Lincoln Town Car. A tall man in a camel-hair coat got out and she kissed his cheek. I recognized him as her father. The two of them stood there talking as Bob Moran approached, giving Seville a big clap on the back like old friends.

Did they work together, I wondered, as I walked back to my office. Did Barbara, who was a sophomore, know Marty Moran, who was two years younger and trying to get into Eastern? I realized I'd never asked Tony Rinaldi what he'd learned about Bob Moran. I made a mental note to call him when I returned to my office, but I didn't have to bother, because he was there waiting for me.

Rochester was still asleep in the corner. "Dog's not doing a very good job of security," Tony said.

"He had a big weekend. How's the investigation going?"

"Not so good. There was nothing unusual in Dagorian's phone records. His email, though, that's another story."

"How so?"

"Tell me about this guy Mike MacCormac. He seems to have exchanged a lot of very angry emails with Dagorian."

"Mike? He's my boss. Ex-football player, very aggressive, very determined. He's the guy with the main responsibility for this big fund-raising campaign we're running. He and Joe used to argue all the time."

I looked at him. "Did Mike threaten him?"

Rinaldi shook his head. "No. Everything was about the college, and this fund-raising campaign. Nothing personal, nothing like a threat. " He sighed. "If this case gets solved, it's going to be through police work. You go on your hunches and you go with the clues, and sometimes you just have to start all over again. Maybe you get a lucky break and you solve a case the first time out, but that's the exception, not the rule."

"You don't get very many homicides here in Leighville."

"No, but we do get drug cases up on the campus, and burglaries and muggings occasionally. You use the same skills to try and solve homicides, but the stakes are higher."

"What ever happened with Bob Moran?" I asked. "You know that after Joe died, his son was offered admission here."

"I'm treading lightly," Tony said. "He's a big cheese in town, you know. Friends with the mayor and the chief of police. I met with him again this morning—told him I wanted to get some background on who was where the night Dagorian was murdered."

"Did he say anything?"

"He didn't confess, if that's what you're asking. But I checked, and his prints are in the FBI's IAFIS database, because he was in the Army in the first Iraq war."

"Do they match the print you got from the knife?"

"Nope."

"But that print could have been from someone else, you know," I said. "Maybe Moran picked up a knife that another guest had used, and made sure to wipe his own prints off, or use gloves."

"You really read too many mysteries," Tony said.

"What was his specialty in the military?" I asked. "Was he trained in how to subdue sentries? Because I read somewhere that the Army trains you to go up behind a sentry and slit his throat, to keep him from making any noise. And that's what happened to Joe, wasn't it? His throat was slit from behind?"

"I don't have access to that kind of information myself," Tony said. "And I have no cause to go searching for it, when his fingerprint doesn't match the one on the knife."

"And it doesn't match anyone in the AIFIS database?"

He shook his head.

"Have you spoken to Ike Arumba?" I asked. "The tall, skinny kid from The Rising Sons?"

He opened his notebook and paged through it. "Nope. Too busy trying to find something on Moran, and going through Dagorian's records."

"Well, maybe you should." I told him about my visit to Verona Santander, and the letter we had found in Joe's file indicating he was going to fire Ike.

"How serious is something like that up here?" he asked. "It's not like the girl didn't consent, though of course there was some implied pressure. But boys have been diddling girls since Adam and Eve."

"We have a strict policy against sexual harassment," I said. "There was a situation a couple of years ago where a girl said she was forced to have sex with a couple of boys at a frat party. The college really cracked down after that."

"I remember that case. I wasn't the investigator, but I know it was hell to get details out of anyone up here."

"I hate to get him into trouble; he seems like a pretty good kid. But you should talk to him."

"Can I get a copy of the letter?"

I buzzed Sally and asked her. "I guess so," she said. "I'll make a copy."

"There's one more thing," I said to Tony, after I hung up the phone. "Does the name Perpetua Kaufman mean anything to you?"

"Sounds like a Jewish saint."

"You're not far off the mark. She was a former nun who taught here at Eastern. She died over winter break. Somebody told me it was a faulty space heater."

"And?"

"And she knew Joe Dagorian. She and Joe were the two leaders of a local ecological organization. It just struck me as strange that both of them would die so close to each other."

"People die every day," he said. "She was an elderly woman, this ex-nun?"

"Yeah."

"We get lots of deaths of elderly people in the winter. Some of them from exposure, some from falls, some, like this lady, from bad space heaters, or carbon monoxide. But you're right, it is a funky kind of coincidence. Spell the name."

I did. "But she lived in Stewart's Crossing. You ought to call Rick Stemper and see what he knows about it."

"I do know how to interface with other law enforcement agencies," Tony said drily. He stood up. "I appreciate your time, and the lead on the kid and the ex-nun. I'll do some checking up on both of them. You never know what I'll find. They say police work is 1% inspiration and 99% perspiration."

"I thought they said that about genius."

"You mean they aren't the same thing?" He smiled, put on his fur hat, and walked out.

Who's A Good Boy?

Soon after Tony left, I heard a heavy, erratic pounding reverberating through Fields Hall. I realized it was coming from the alumni and development office, next door to mine. I pushed the door open and saw Mike MacCormac standing in his office, punching the wall. He looked up in mid-punch, saw me standing there, and laughed uncomfortably.

"Good strong walls," he said. "Did you hear me?"

"Uh-huh. What's the matter?"

"You know, typical frustrations. I just, uh, can't let it build up inside me, you know? Otherwise it makes me crazy. So I take it out on my wall, sometimes on the floor. Sometimes I go over to the gym and borrow a punching bag."

I struggled to find something to say, looking around the office for inspiration. On the floor at my feet was a doctor's prescription, and I picked it up and placed it on his desk. As I did, I noticed that it was for Viagra. I wondered what a young guy like him was doing with a drug for erectile dysfunction, but didn't want to say anything. I didn't want him turning his aggression against me.

"You've got a lot of responsibility. You can't let it get to you. " I shrugged. "Take it easy on the wall, or we'll be sharing a suite of offices."

As I walked out I passed Juan and Jose, the football players. Why were they always hanging around Mike's office? Was it just that he had been a football player? Shouldn't they be buddying up with Sam Boni instead? They didn't seem to be work-study students, because I never actually saw them working.

I went back to my office and checked my email, where I saw a response to my message to Lili. My hand shaking a little, I clicked the mouse to open it. "It was nice to run into a familiar face in the big bad city," she wrote. "We'll have to get together again sometime around Leighville."

Well. What did that mean? How did people start dating again, at forty-three? Did I have the patience for the delicate dance of getting to know you, or for figuring out symbols and codes I hadn't thought about since my post-college dating days?

I looked to Rochester for advice, but he was still asleep. I wasn't quite desperate enough to call Tor or Rick and ask advice, so instead I stewed around in my office, unable to concentrate on much.

Dezhanne stuck her head in my door as I was trying to put together a press release on an ecological awareness program the biology department was sponsoring. "I'm clocking out. By the way, I aced my organic midterm. You know, the one I was stressing about last week."

"So the pre-med thing is back on?"

"Until the final exam," she said and walked out, her curls bouncing.

I looked over to where Rochester lay, and as if he sensed my gaze on him, he looked up, yawned, then stood up and came over to me. "Who's a good boy?" I asked, scratching behind his ears.

He jumped up and put his paws on my groin, nearly knocking me over. "All right, I get the hint," I said. "It's time for us to go home."

I struggled with him to get his leash on, and once I had him hooked up, he took off toward the office door, dragging me behind him. I had to struggle to lock the door behind us, with him tugging the leash forward.

As we drove home along the River Road, darkness falling around us, I thought about Joe Dagorian again. There were so many problems swirling around him—his opposition to the capital campaign, his possible corruption or incompetence in the building of the gym, his resistance to granting admission to Bob Moran's son. And now the possibility that there was something going on with the Bucks County Nature Conservancy.

Add to that the statistics Joe had been fudging. If he released them, the effect on Eastern's reputation could be disastrous. That kind of dishonesty wasn't tolerated well in academia, and there were a lot of competing institutions that would jump on the issue and use it against us.

When we got home, I took Rochester for a quick walk, then fed him his dinner and sat down at my laptop. I had been a good boy for a long time, not snooping in places I wasn't supposed to go, meeting all Santiago Santos's requirements. But I wondered if there was something I could find out myself, something Rinaldi might not be able to discover.

I began with the Bucks County Nature Conservancy. An internet search revealed a number of mentions of the group on websites and in the local paper, and I read them all. Most of them were simple things like meeting notices, but there was an extensive article in the Courier-Times about a developer's plans for a tract of undeveloped land along the Tohickon Creek, and opposition toward the plans from Joe's group.

A development company called Bar-Lyn Investments wanted to build an assisted living facility for the elderly along the creek. The BCNC was concerned about the loss of habitat for various kinds of flora and fauna, as well as the damage from construction and increased vehicle traffic through the area.

In early January, Joe had spoken up at a zoning meeting against reclassifying the zoning from agricultural to a residential category that would allow adult congregate living, and the commission had agreed to table Bar-Lyn's request pending an evaluation of the ecological consequences.

I followed a link to Bar-Lyn's website, and discovered that it was a real estate development company based in Upper Bucks County, which built and operated several small shopping centers. The ACLF was its biggest project, and a statement on the company's home page indicated it hoped the zoning problem would be solved quickly so that construction could proceed.

I was intrigued, so I did some more searching on Bar-Lyn Investments. I found that each of the small shopping centers the company owned was heavily mortgaged—always a bad sign, especially in this economy. Searching for commercial property, I found that there were vacancies at all of Bar-Lyn's centers.

I looked up the property records for Joe's house, and the land he co-owned with Norah in New Hampshire. I didn't care enough to try to hack into the property appraiser's database, just checked the public records.

I reread Perpetua's obituary, looking for clues to her death, but there were none. I felt like I was grasping at straws, at something that was just out of reach. Before I could get myself into real trouble, snooping around her bank account or credit card records, I called Rick. "How's the Rascal doing?"

"He figured out how to open the door to the downstairs bathroom where I keep the laundry basket. By the time I got home I found socks and underwear all over the place."

"I told you, you need a crate for him," I said. "Rochester doesn't need his any more. Why don't I bring it over?"

"Want to bring a pizza with it?"

I realized I hadn't eaten dinner and I was starving. "You buy, I fly," I said.

"Deal. I'll order it from Piece A' Pizza. You can swing by on your way down here."

When I was growing up in Stewart's Crossing, there wasn't much in the way of ethnic food, and it all came out of the restaurant owner's family tradition. We drove into the Chambersburg section of Trenton, the Italian neighborhood, to Roman Hall for pasta and pizza. We ate Greek food at the Starlight Diner in Levittown, owned by the Pappases. We picked up bagels from Abe's, owned by an elderly man who went to the same synagogue we did.

Now, the ethnicities were all mixed up. Pakistanis owned the pizza parlor, and Israelis the French café in Newtown. The old places where my family had eaten when I was growing up were gone, replaced by Pan-Asian cuisine, chain Mexican and Italian restaurants, and vegan and vegetarian cafés I didn't know who owned any of them.

I had taken Rochester's crate apart and stored it in the garage, leaning up against a wall on the passenger side of the BMW. I opened the garage door, dragged the crate around and propped it in the trunk, and tied it closed with a bungee cord.

I made Rochester get in the back seat, which he didn't like. He kept sticking his long snout over the back of my seat and sniffing at my neck. And when I picked up the pizza, a large Sicilian cut with mushrooms, sausage and meatballs, he kept trying to nose open the box on the seat next to me. "No," I said, elbowing him in the snout.

He sat back on the seat to pout. "You'll get yours when we get to Rick's."

Rick came out to help me unload the BMW. "Spoke to your buddy Tony Rinaldi today," he said. Though it was forty degrees outside, he was wearing a pair of Hawaiian-print shorts and a T-shirt that read "Dial 9-1-1. Make a cop come."

Rascal came charging out behind him, as he lifted the pizza box from the front seat. "He said you're interested in Sister Perpetua," he said.

Rochester leaped through the gap between the two front seats and out the front door before I could even get the back door open.

"Why does everyone call her that?" I asked. "I thought she gave up being a nun when she got married."

"Don't know. That's what everybody I talked to called her." The two dogs raced each other around the car as I lifted the crate out, then slammed the trunk closed.

"Rochester. Sit," I said. He skidded to a stop, then plopped his butt on the gravel of Rick's driveway. Rascal stared at him, remaining on all fours.

"How do you get him to do that?" Rick asked.

"Training. Rascal. Sit. " I pointed to the pavement next to Rochester.

Rascal nosed at Rochester's ass, and Rochester gave him a short woof. Rascal looked up at both of us, then sat down next to Rochester. Rick shook his head in amazement.

"After dinner I'll show you some of the things I do with Rochester," I said. "Come on, boys, let's go in the house."

They hopped up and followed us in. Rick and I sat down at the table and began to eat. Absently he peeled off a piece of crust and went to hand it to Rascal. "Don't just give it to him," I said. "Make him work for it."

"What?"

"Give it to me. " He handed me the crust and I looked down at Rascal, who was sitting on his haunches next to us. "Rascal. Down." I pointed to the floor. He just turned his head toward me.

"Rochester. Down." I repeated the motion, and Rochester sprawled down to the floor. I handed him the piece of crust, which he wolfed down greedily.

Then I peeled another piece of crust off, and repeated the instructions to Rascal. This time he knew what to do, and he followed Rochester's lead.

"Amazing," Rick said, shaking his head.

"It's about making a connection with the dog."

We ate for a while, sometimes giving the dogs food with commands, sometimes not. By the time we finished, they were sprawled on the floor, snoozing, both of them the picture of indolence.

"So tell me why you think someone murdered Sister Perpetua," Rick said.

I told him what I had learned about the connection between her and Joe Dagorian, the Bucks County Nature Conservancy and Bar-Lyn Development.

"Nobody's cleaned out her house yet," he said. "I'll have to get a search warrant and impound the space heater, see if anyone's tampered with it."

He opened up a half-gallon of Neapolitan ice cream and hogged the strawberry, and I told him about Liliana Weinstock. "You're dating a doctor," he said, in a heavy Jewish accent. "Your mother would be so proud."

"Just one date so far. And one kiss."

When I finished my ice cream, I took Rochester home, where I spent some time stroking his golden flanks, putting my efforts were they were most appreciated.

Turning up the Heat

When Rochester and I woke up the next morning, we found that an overnight snowfall had reimagined Stewart's Crossing for us. Familiar rooftops and trees were reshaped in white, driveways and sidewalks were covered over, and the cars parked along our street were blanketed five or six inches under.

I let Rochester out in the front yard to pee, and he stained the white snow bright yellow around the corner of the house. Then we went back inside to wait until the streets of River Bend had been plowed, which pleased Rochester, because I spent most of the time lying on the floor rubbing his belly and telling him what a good dog he was.

Once the plow had passed, I suited up in my thermal long johns, ski pants, long-sleeved T-shirt, and down parka. I dug my LL Bean duck boots out of the back of the closet put on two layers of socks, and strapped myself in. Then I wrapped a cashmere scarf around my neck, pulled on my insulated gloves and my wooly hat, and we went for his morning walk. He swam and dove through the drifts as I stuck to the asphalt. A couple of my neighbors had already shoveled their cars out, but a lot looked like they were staying in.

My father had a saying about snow. "God brought it, and God will take it away. " That didn't prevent him from assigning me to shovel the driveway, though. I wished I had brought a camera, or at least my cell phone, because Rochester looked so adorable covered in a light coating of snow, the white crystals glistening against his golden fur. When he ran, his ears flapped up, making him look like a space alien dog. He emerged from one drift with a big glob of snow just behind his nose, and he kept shaking his head trying to dislodge it.

By the time we circled back to the townhouse, I was exhausted, but Rochester was still full of vigor, flopping on his back in the snow and wiggling around, making his own kind of snow angel. "What the hell," I said, dropping his leash and flopping down next to him. I spread my arms and flapped, and then Rochester crawled on top of me, sniffing and licking my chin until I couldn't stop laughing and had to push him off me.

I shed my boots, socks, and many layers on my way through the living room, grabbing a towel from the laundry room to clean the road salt from between Rochester's paws. Then I grabbed another couple of towels and dried him off. It would have gone more smoothly if he hadn't kept shaking on me, but that's Rochester.

A good hot shower rejuvenated me. Rochester was under the bed and wouldn't come out until I stood downstairs by the front door threatening to leave without him.

The snow was piled high along the streets and sidewalks throughout the campus. There were still beautiful, virgin patches between buildings, but students were already sledding down the back side of the hill, slaloming between pine trees. I even saw one kid on cross-country skis heading toward Blair Hall. I had to hold Rochester on a tight leash to keep him from romping through the drifts the way he had back in River Bend.

I saw Mike in the kitchen around eleven when I went down for a cup of coffee. He was wearing an oversized crimson sweatshirt with a big white H on it over his shirt and tie. "I've called Physical Plant three times," he said. "There's something wrong with the heat in my office and I'm freezing in there."

"I didn't know you went to Harvard," I said, pointing at the sweatshirt.

"I didn't," Mike said. "But I went to a fund-raising conference there once. Harvard is just the ideal of fund-raising. I mean, it's the Harvard of fund-raising. " He laughed a little at his own joke. "So I bought this sweatshirt, sort of like something to aspire to."

I found it hard to understand aspiring to a sweatshirt, but I didn't say anything. I got my coffee and went back to my office.

Tony Rinaldi stopped by my office just before noon. "Hey," I said. "I had dinner with Rick last night. He's

148

going to get a search warrant for Perpetua Kaufman's house."

"Thanks for the update," he said, pushing Rochester's nose away from his crotch. "But just so you know, we police guys do communicate with each other."

"Good to know my police dollars are at work. Have you gotten hold of Ike Arumba?"

"Apparently his singing group was performing at a concert in New Haven," Tony said. "He's coming down to the station this afternoon for a chat. I'd like to find out what he has to say about that letter Dagorian wrote. And I'd like to talk to him some more about what he might have seen or heard outside that night. It's possible he heard something, but because of the dope connection he didn't want to speak up."

"It's almost noon," I said. "You want to get some lunch?"

"Sure. Even policemen have to eat. "

I told Rochester I would bring something back for him, and Tony and I walked outside, where a mass of gray clouds had taken over the sky. "Looks kind of grim," he said. "Instead of walking into town, why don't we drive somewhere. There's a pretty good deli around the back side of the hill. You feel like a sandwich?" He held up his hand. "And I promise not to say you don't look like one."

We walked quickly to his car, breathing icicles, and he drove us around to the industrial part of town, where I'd met the homeless man outside the printer's. "I have to say, I haven't spent much time in this end of town," I said when we were seated at a counter looking at the menu. "Even when I was in school, I spent most of my time up on the campus."

"I guess any school is like that," Tony said. He closed his menu and put it down on top of the paper placemat. "Look at me. Lived my whole life in Leighville and never went up to the campus more than half a dozen times."

The waitress took our orders and Tony said, "So what's your theory on this case? Come on, I know you've got one."

"I don't know," I said. I picked a pickle out of a dish on the counter and started to munch on it. "There are so many sides to this case. First you thought it was a personal motive—that Norah Leedom killed him because of that land deal. Then all the possible college issues—Joe's arguments with Mike MacCormac, the problems getting Bob Moran's son admitted. Now there's this possible complication with Perpetua Kaufman. Joe could have been killed for some reason we don't even know about."

"I'm glad to see you're keeping an open mind. Did Rick tell you anything new about Perpetua Kaufman?"

"Because she died at home, without a physician present, she had to be autopsied," Tony said. "I looked up the results. Carbon monoxide poisoning, just like you thought. Cause was supposed to be a faulty space heater."

"Rick said he's going to go over to her house. If there's anything strange about the space heater, I'm sure he'll find it."

Our sandwiches arrived, and I told him what I'd discovered about Bar-Lyn Investments. "It sounds like the company's in trouble, and they've got a lot invested in this project. Joe and Perpetua were protesting against it—and now they're both dead."

"You have a vivid imagination, you know that, Steve?" he said. "Between Rick and me, we'll see what's going on."

We ate our sandwiches, talking about mortgages and dogs and the lousy winter weather, and for a little while we forgot about Joe Dagorian and his murder. I ordered an extra plain hamburger patty for Rochester, which the waitress brought over in a little styrofoam box.

We finished, split the check, and he dropped me back off at Fields Hall. "Take care," I said. "Let me know when anything develops."

I fed Rochester his burger in chunks. "Watch my fingers," I said. "Daddy is not on the menu."

Looking out the French doors of my office later that afternoon, I saw Ike Arumba walking through the snow,

150

his head down, and I wondered what had happened with Tony Rinaldi. But I was too busy putting together a couple of alumni profiles for Mike to give it much thought.

Sally stuck her head in my door just before five o'clock, when things in Fields Hall were winding down before the weekend. "Got a minute?"

"Sure. " I motioned her to a seat across from me.

"I'm dead," she said. "What a week. Four high school visits, a meeting of the alumni council on admissions, and a college fair in Scranton that went on for hours. Babson is hounding me about interviewing candidates for my old job, and I'm having trouble finding a temp who can answer the phone without acting like a total moron."

She sighed. "And I talked to Ike. I told him I was very disturbed by Verona Santander's allegations, and that I had found the letter in Joe's file, and that I was going to have to let him go."

"How did he take it?" I remembered seeing him walk and wondered if that was what had upset him, not the visit to the Leighville police.

"Not well. Basically he made some threats."

I was surprised. I'd never taken Ike for the violent kind. "He threatened you?"

"Not physically. But he said he knew a lot about what had been going on in the admissions office and if I fired him he would, as he said, 'let people know. '"

"Do you think he really knows anything?"

She nodded. "He certainly made it seem like he did. He mentioned the possibility that our statistics weren't correct. And that as Joe's assistant, I'd have to take the fall."

She started to cry. "It's true, you know. Even though I didn't have anything to do with faking the data, Babson will take it out on me."

"I think he'd have to. The publicity would be damning and he'd have to demonstrate that he's doing something to make a change."

"It's not fair." She pulled a tissue from the pocket of her plaid skirt and dabbed at her eyes.

151

"Does Ike want anything besides his job?" I asked.

"A letter of recommendation."

"I read somewhere that your brain isn't fully developed when you're a teenager," I said. "And the part that's slowest to develop is the part that understands things like the consequences of your actions. " I sat back in my chair. "Though in my case that part still doesn't work that well."

"Are you saying I should give in to him?"

"We're the adults, so let's try and look at this rationally," I said. "Let's say you stick to your guns and fire him. He tells Babson, or the press, what he knows about the fudged statistics. Joe's reputation is shot, and Eastern gets a lot of nasty media attention. For sure, our last-minute admissions go down, and our yield goes down, too. Who wants to go to a college under a cloud of scandal?"

"You think it would be that bad?"

"Worse. You'd lose your job, too. Even though you did nothing wrong. And it would be really hard for you to get another admissions job, or any job at a college, with something like that circling around you."

She started crying again. "Why do you think Joe changed those statistics in the first place, Steve? I mean, he loved Eastern. Why would he do something to jeopardize it?"

"Maybe he thought he was helping. Suppose applications were down one year, but Joe thought they'd pick up. So he invented a few extra and things looked just as good. But then the next year they were down further, and he couldn't reverse the statistics from the year before, so he invented even more. He probably kept hoping things would improve from year to year, and when they didn't it was harder and harder to tell the truth."

"So he kept on inventing and upgrading applications," Sally said. "Well, we'll never know the real reason now."

"I think the issue of Ike is tied up with what we think of Joe, too," I said. "Suppose Ike really is innocent, and Joe trumped it up for his own reasons. I don't think either you or I believe what Ike did was criminal—it was just poor judgment. Even threatening you—that's just a kid who doesn't know what else to do. And I don't think either of us wants to see Joe, or Eastern, go down in flames."

"So I let him keep his job."

"I'll write the letter of recommendation for you, if you want."

"I might take you up on that." She stood up. "Well, I have to get back to work."

I found myself yawning. I thought I'd better get one last cup of coffee from the kitchen before trying to drive back to Stewart's Crossing in the dark. That's when I ran into Ike Arumba.

He Made A Mistake

"Say, Mr. Levitan, do you think I could talk to you for a couple of minutes?" Ike asked. "I know you're friendly with Sally, and I was figuring maybe you could help me out."

"Why don't we go back to my office? We'll have a little more privacy that way."

He nodded and followed me out. "Pretty cold out today, isn't it?" I said. He nodded. I tried again. "Well, it'll be spring soon, and you'll be graduating-- no more Leighville winters."

This time he looked actively miserable. We got into my office, where the space heater I had turned on earlier had made some progress. Rochester, though, was still sprawled by the French doors, his back against the glass. I couldn't understand how he liked that cold against his skin—but then, there are a lot of things about that dog I still don't understand.

I motioned Ike to the chair across from my desk, and we both sat. "What can I do to help you?"

"Well, it's kind of hard to explain."

Rochester got up from his place by the French doors and walked over to Ike, putting his head in Ike's lap. Ike began to stroke his head.

"I'm the one who spoke to Verona Santander. Her story sounded pretty credible. But I believe there are always two sides, and I'm willing to listen to yours if you want."

"She's nuts, that girl, you know?" he said quickly. "I mean, she was cute, and she seemed pretty bright, and she asked a lot of good questions about Eastern and she seemed real interested."

I nodded.

"So then after my program was over she came up and said, well, if I was eating all alone and looking for some company, she could show me a good place to go. We went to this restaurant, and we had a really nice dinner and a good conversation, and she said her parents were out of town and did I want to come over for a little while."

His shoulders slumped and he looked ready to cry. Rochester snuffled against his hand. "Yes?" I said as gently as I could.

"Well, I thought it was out of line, you know, but then I said, what the hell? I mean, I was all by myself in town and otherwise I would just go back to my hotel room and watch TV. So we went over there, and she started coming on to me. I mean, I know high school girls and all, but she was pretty advanced. She was, like, stroking my leg and all, and well, you know how a guy gets like that."

I couldn't help smiling a little. "I understand."

"You see I couldn't talk about this to Sally. I just couldn't say it." Rochester sensed the crisis was over, and he slumped down on the floor next to Ike.

"So anyway she was really coming on to me and I knew it was wrong to do but I just couldn't help myself. So we did it and then after a while I went back to my hotel room and went to sleep, and when I got back I put a good write-up on her into her file. Not because of that night or anything, but she was a smart girl and she wanted to go to Eastern, and that's what I said. I mean, if you've met her and talked to her you can see it was the truth."

"I'll take a look in her file." I made a note on the pad next to my phone.

"Oh, sure, please. There's nothing there I'd want to hide. So anyway she wrote me a nice note after I got home, and I put it in the file, and then we admitted her and she wrote me another note and asked why I didn't answer the first one. So I wrote her back and thanked her for her notes and said we looked forward to having her at Eastern in the fall. I was trying to be real careful, see, to keep it from developing into anything."

"I see."

"A copy of my note is in the file. So then she sent me a real nasty note and said she was going to Barnard where they respected her as a woman. So I said, hey, this comes from left field, and I put it in the file and I

155

forgot about her. The next thing I know, maybe six months later, old Joe starts to get real cold to me and I don't know why. So then at that party, the bunch of us guys were standing around outside, smoking, you know, and old Joe came up and told me that he could tell I didn't have a good moral character, if I was, you know, getting high."

Rochester rolled over on his back and started waving his legs. I got up and found one of his rawhide bones next to the file cabinet, and stuck it into his mouth.

"When we were talking old Joe brought up the whole thing with Verona, and said that he had written a letter to President Babson back when it happened, and he'd been holding on to it, but now, you know, he was going to send it. I mean, like, he hadn't even talked to me about it, and here he was writing to the President that I should be expelled."

Rochester ground away at the bone as Ike shivered. "Expelled! And I've only got the rest of this semester. I mean, it was bad enough that he didn't want to give me a job after graduation-- we had only talked about it a little, nothing was firmed up, but I was counting on it. It just freaked me out."

He stopped. "Hey, how did you know to talk to Verona? Did old Joe tell you?"

"Joe gave a Xerox of the note to Sally to review before he sent it. She asked me to talk to Verona when I was in New York this past weekend." I looked at him. "Did you argue with Joe the night of the party?"

He nodded. "I mean, it was bad timing and all, but I guess I was a little buzzed, and I wasn't really thinking. I just wanted to find out what was going on. Finally he said we would talk about it the next day and I said OK and I went back inside."

Rochester stood up with his rawhide bone in his mouth and walked back over to his place by the French doors. I looked beyond him at the snowy landscape. "Did you see anyone else out in the garden?"

To Save A Career

I collected my stuff and walked down to Sally's office, but she had already left for the day. Rochester and I walked back to the parking lot, and I while he stopped to sniff and pee I looked around and marveled at how pretty the campus was blanketed in white. I loved the collegiate Gothic style of the architecture, all the arched entrances and tall buildings with spires.

Several of the older buildings had huge wooden doors with iron handles, often with leaded glass windows inserted. Ivy crawled up the stone walls and pine trees stood sentinel at many entrances. I was less fond of the modern buildings on campus, which seemed to be built of soul-crushing concrete, without the higher aspirations of the older buildings.

The car was cold, and I kept one hand on Rochester for warmth until the heater kicked in. He didn't seem to mind. When we got home, we took another long, snowy walk, and I felt invigorated by the cold.

I missed the snow when I lived in California. Mary and I had gone skiing in Tahoe once, but she wasn't really a cold-weather kind of gal. I wondered how Rochester would like cross-country skiing. I'd tried it once, years before, in Vermont, and I liked it. I was thinking maybe I could give it a go again. Maybe with Rick, Rochester and Rascal romping along beside us.

Then Rochester pulled so hard on his leash that I nearly fell forward, and I reconsidered that plan.

The townhouse my father had left me suited us both pretty well, though the one thing it was missing was a fireplace. I wished Rochester and I could have dried off in front of a nice, crackling fire, but instead I pulled out the last towels and dried him off, then ran a load of laundry. He crawled under my bed to lick himself in private places, and I sat up and read a mystery novel, trying to ignore the feeling that I was inside one myself.

The next morning, Rochester and I walked into Fields Hall just before nine. My cell phone began to ring, and I had to struggle to pull off a glove and find the

159

phone in my pocket. Rochester must have sniffed something across the lobby, perhaps some discarded tidbit, and he tried to tug me over there.

"Hold on, dog," I said, grabbing the phone just before the call went to voice mail.

Rochester kept pulling, and I had to yank hard on his leash. I answered the call, which turned out to be a wrong number.

I finally let Rochester have his head, and he went right over to the metal bin which contained copies of The Eastern *Daily Sun*, the campus newspaper, and sat down.

I picked up a copy of the paper, remembering Ike's admission that he'd leaked some information to a girl he knew who wrote for the paper, and once I'd done so Rochester stood up and headed down the hall.

Juggling his leash and the paper, I opened the front page. The headline at the bottom of the page was "Are we really as good as we think we are?"

My heart sank as I hurried behind Rochester to my office. I kicked off my boots and unhooked his leash, and he walked over to his place by the French doors. As I unreeled my scarf and shrugged out of my coat, I skimmed the article.

Fortunately the reporter, Rose Hippz, didn't make any concrete allegations. She just hinted that there were irregularities in the admissions office, and wondered if things would be changing now that Joe Dagorian was gone.

I buzzed Sally, but the receptionist said she was at a school visit that morning. And Babson's secretary said that he was having breakfast with a group of wealthy alumni and wasn't expected in the office until eleven.

My next call was to Tony Rinaldi. After a few preliminaries he came on the line. "I think we're making some progress," he said. "Your friend Mr. Arumba was awfully unhappy about speaking to me."

"You just have a way with people."

He laughed. "Well, I'll tell you, I didn't like some of his answers. More than that, I didn't like his attitude. He was definitely trying to hide something."

"Did you confront him about that girl in New York?"

"Uh-huh. That's when he really got scared. He denied the incident, he denied that Dagorian had ever confronted him about it. He denied even being out in the garden that night."

"Can't blame him for that. Smoking dope is still illegal in Pennsylvania, isn't it?"

"I'm not trying to put a couple of college kids behind bars for getting high," he said. "I'm looking for a murderer."

"If it matters, he confessed everything to me," I said. "But he swears Joe was alive when he went back into Fields Hall."

"I wish I could put this case to bed, but I need more than a jittery kid who denies everything to make an arrest. I've got some boys on it, though. I told him not to go anywhere without telling us."

I told him about Ike's threat, and how desperate he was to hold on to his job in the admissions office. "That's a motive," Tony said. "Listen, gotta go. Talk to you later."

Sally came into my office as I was hanging up. "How was your school visit?" I asked.

"Not good. All anyone wanted to talk about was crime and murder. A couple of kids even said their parents would never let them go to Eastern after what happened."

"Ike Arumba cried on my shoulder yesterday afternoon," I said. "In his version of what happened in Portland between him and Verona Santander, she comes off as a teenaged temptress and he's her innocent victim. Of course, he knows what he did was wrong, but he's not really willing to accept much of the blame."

"You believe him over Verona?"

"I think the truth is somewhere between both stories," I said. "But I think it's close enough to Ike's version to warrant giving him a second chance. I'd like to take a look at Verona's file and see if what he told me matches up with what's in there."

"Did you see the *Daily Sun* this morning?"

"Yeah. He told me yesterday that was going to happen. But I think if you back off, he will, too."

"Steve."

"Wait, Sally, before you make up your mind. Remember he's just a kid, and you might be taking his whole career away from him before he starts, just for one mistake. A bad mistake, all right, but he wants you to let him prove himself again. He really wants to work in admissions and he wants you to let him try and show you he's a decent guy."

"You must have believed him," Sally said.

"Well, yeah, and I've made a few mistakes myself. I'd hate to see him suffer so much for just one."

"I kind of like him myself," she said. "We hit it off right away, what with both of us coming from the Northwest. I probably should give him a second chance. And as you say, if I keep him away from the candidates, he doesn't have much room to screw up."

"Excuse the pun," I said. We both laughed. "He also told me Joe was recommending to Babson that he be expelled, and he confronted Joe in the garden and they argued."

Sally's mouth dropped open. "Do you think Ike killed him?"

"Ike had a powerful motive. But the killer used a knife from the kitchen, and Ike didn't know Joe was considering having him expelled until they talked outside."

"He could have had the knife with him."

"Why?"

"I don't know. Maybe he just did." Sally stood up. "I'll pull out Verona's file for you. Meanwhile I've got to get back to wade through everything that came in this morning."

I grabbed lunch at the Cafette, unwilling to go too far in the cold, and was glad when it was time to head to the tech writing class. When I walked into the classroom, I saw Lou Segusi sitting at a computer, trying to type one-handed with his left hand. His right arm was in a cast.

"What happened to you?" I asked.

162

"Had a little accident. But I can't let it slow me down. I've got a lot of papers to finish over the next few weeks."

"Why don't you just ask for extensions? Any professor can see it's tough for you to type like that."

He shook his head. "Then I'll just get farther behind."

"What are you majoring in, Lou?"

"English. I want to be a professional writer when I graduate. Not a novelist or anything—I'm not that creative. I just like to write. I'm thinking I could get a job as a technical writer or work for a magazine. That's why I wanted to take this course."

"I was a tech writer myself for a long time. I'd be happy to talk about it with you sometime."

"Would you, Mr. Levitan? That would be great. I'm graduating this term and I don't really know where to look for jobs."

"You have time tomorrow afternoon?" I asked. "Say, two o'clock? Come over to my office in Fields Hall and we'll do some brainstorming."

"Cool. My parents will be so relieved if they see I have some kind of direction."

I launched the class into more discussion of their research papers, and then I set them loose for research and writing. As I watched Lou peck away at the computer, once again I wondered how many papers this kid had to write in a term. I was an English major myself, and most of what I had to do when I was a student was read—novels and short story collections and anthologies and reference books. Sure, I had to write papers, too, but usually just a couple each semester.

There was something hinky about him, I decided. I wasn't sure what it was, but I was going to do some probing the next day when we met in my office.

Bad Dog!

I met Tony Rinaldi on the way to my office. Tony patted his head absently, then closed my office door. "I'm close to making an arrest in Dagorian's murder," he said, sitting down across from me. "I wanted to give you a heads up."

"Terrific! Give me the scoop."

"It's our friend Mr. Arumba. We've got him in the right place at the right time, and we know he and Dagorian argued, and that Dagorian was threatening to have him expelled."

My heart sank. "I had a long talk with Ike yesterday, and I don't think he did it."

"Convince me, then."

I related my conversation with Ike Arumba to him. "I don't see how he could have gotten the knife. Does his fingerprint match the one on the knife?"

He frowned. "No. That's the one detail that doesn't fit."

"The other detail that doesn't is that Ike had no motive to kill Joe until they had their confrontation in the garden."

"He could have run inside to get the knife, and then come back and killed him."

"I saw him come inside, and just a couple of minutes later he was on stage. He didn't have time to find a knife, go back outside, kill Joe, and then get into place with the rest of the singers. And what about Perpetua Kaufman? Did you hear from Rick Stemper if anyone tampered with the space heater?"

He sighed. "It looks like the flue was blocked with an accumulation of dust and lint. That caused a buildup of carbon monoxide, and it accumulated in Mrs. Kaufman's bedroom. She was particularly at risk because she was elderly and had some respiratory problems."

"So she was murdered?"

"That's harder to prove. Rick's expert said the stuff blocking the flue was packed in pretty well, and it's hard

164

for it to accumulate naturally like that. He tested the heater for fingerprints and the only ones on it were Mrs. Kaufman's. But the back of the unit had been wiped clean."

"Don't you see?" I said. "If Perpetua Kaufman and Joe Dagorian were both murdered, then there has to be a connection between them. And Ike Arumba can't be that connection."

"How do you know, Steve? How do you know he didn't have a beef with her in a class, or that Dagorian told her about his plans to have the kid expelled?"

I blew out a big breath. "But you and Rick could check those things out, right?"

"Yes. We could. And we will."

He left, and I resisted the urge to call Rick Stemper and get his take on things. Tony was already cranky with me, and I didn't want him to think I was going around behind his back because I didn't trust him to do things right. Instead I walked down the hall to Sally's office. "Rinaldi wants to arrest Ike for Joe's murder," I said. "But I don't think he did it, and I feel like I need to do something. Can I see Verona's application folder? I want to be sure the documentation says what Ike told me."

Sally handed me a file from her desk. "I pulled this out of the archives for you. I looked through it myself, and it does seem like Ike was very careful to document all his correspondence with her."

"You know, Steve, I want to believe Ike is innocent of everything but it's hard to do. I can even understand why he might have killed Joe. Joe could have ruined his entire academic career."

"Well, it may be a motive for murder but it's not an excuse," I said. "And we can't use it to put an innocent person away. Before I see that kid go to jail I'm going to be sure that he's guilty."

When I got back to my office, there were papers scattered all over the floor, and Rochester was sitting right in the middle of them, a goofy grin on his face.

"Rochester!" I said. "Bad dog!"

I started collecting the papers and organizing them once more. Rochester refused to budge until I had picked up everything around him. Only then did he get up, stretch, and then walk over to his accustomed spot by the French doors.

That's when I saw what he had been lying on. It was Barbara Seville's admissions folder, including the photos she had submitted as demonstration of her artwork.

Shooting Stars

I read Verona Santander's file, and everything was as Ike had said it would be. So whose story was most believable?

I pushed that idea ahead and read the material on Barbara Seville, the blonde pixie from my tech writing class. In her essay, she mentioned her father and his business, Bar-Lyn Investments, and how she loved to spend time with him out on his construction sites.

Bar-Lyn? Wasn't that the company Joe and Perpetua were fighting against? I turned back to my computer and pulled up the Bar-Lyn website. There was no mention of who owned the company. But then I did a search for the site's registration, and found that Richard Seville was the contact for Bar-Lyn's domain.

I went back to the small photo album she had included with her portfolio. It was divided into sections. The first documented construction at one of her father's sites, a shopping center. I thought she had a good eye for composition, but I wasn't any kind of judge. The second section were portraits—young people who were probably her friends or family members, then a series of elderly people from a nursing or retirement home.

The final section were nature shots. She favored close-ups of algae, lichen, flowers, leaves, and water flowing over stone.

But why had Joe kept this portfolio at home, when it should have been filed at Eastern? The Bucks County Nature Conservancy had been fighting against her father's plans for the property along Tohickon Creek. Was there some connection to her essay, or her portfolio?

Before I could think about it too much I looked up Lili's office phone number on the Eastern website and dialed. "Fine Arts, Dr. Weinstock," she answered.

"Lili? It's Steve Berman. I was wondering if I could show you some photographs from a student's admission portfolio and get your opinion."

"I could use a break," she said. "I've been writing grant requests for an exhibition I want to mount in the fall."

"Maybe I can help you with that."

"Sounds like a good tradeoff. I need to stretch my legs—where's your office?"

I told her, and a few minutes later she was knocking lightly on the frame of my office door.

Usually Rochester is quick to jump up and interrogate any visitor, but he remained slouched in the corner. "Come on in," I said.

"That must be your dog. What's his name—Rickenbacker? Rockefeller?"

"Rochester. He's very friendly. Come on in."

She looked toward him, but he pointedly ignored her, putting his paw over his head, in his typical "If I can't see you, you're not there," move.

"These are the photos I wanted to show you," I said, as she came over to my desk. She pulled the visitor's chair next to mine and sat down.

She didn't say anything for a couple of minutes. I sat there, inhaling the light scent of her perfume, noticing the butterfly pins that kept her masses of hair in check.

"She has a good idea for composition," Lili said at last. "And there's real empathy in her portraits, particularly of the elderly. The nature photos are a bit arty for my taste, but she clearly understands light and shadow and shutter speed."

She leaned back. "Was that what you wanted to know?"

"I don't know. " I explained the situation, from Joe's opposition to her father's company to the fact that he'd kept this material at his home instead of in the admissions archive.

"Let me see the booklet again. " She paged back to the nature photos. "Have you looked into these captions?"

Under each photo was what I assumed was the Latin name of the algae, flower, grass or fern. "Hadn't thought of it. But there's always Google."

168

With Lili spelling, I began researching the items Barbara Seville had photographed. When we came to *Cymophyllus fraserianus,* I discovered that it was a showy perennial called the Common Shooting Star. It grew no taller than half a meter, with white, lavender or lilac flowers that pointed upwards and backwards. It was only found in Somerset County, in the western part of the state.

"That's pretty far away from here," Lili said.

Lili brought out a magnifying glass from her shoulder bag. The photos Barbara had taken of it didn't quite match the ones we found on line. Lili began pointing out very tiny differences in the shape of leaves. "Could she have digitally altered the pictures?" I asked.

"Doubtful," she said. "You'd have to be a very skilled artist to make everything match so carefully, and I haven't seen evidence of that level of artistry anywhere else in the portfolio. And why would she go to that much trouble?"

"If this plant was supposed to be in the western part of the state, and she found some here in Bucks County, would that make it an endangered species, do you think?"

"I'm in Fine Arts, not Natural Sciences," she said. "But it does tie into the protests you said Joe Dagorian was making."

"And Perpetua Kaufman," I said. "Both of them were working to stop Seville's construction plans. And both of them are dead."

Lili pushed her chair back. "This is the point when I go back to my boring grant applications."

"Thanks, Lili. This was really helpful. " We both stood up at the same time, and for a brief moment our faces were close enough for a kiss. But I hesitated, and you know what they say about those who hesitate. All is lost.

But I screwed up my courage before she walked out the door and said, "Maybe I could come over sometime and help you with those grant applications. Or maybe we could... have dinner again. Friday night?"

"That would be great," she said. "We'll talk Friday and make plans. " On her way out the door she stopped next to Rochester and reached down to scratch behind his ears. "See you later, sweet boy."

I kind of hoped she was talking to me, but probably not. Rochester did not respond, and she walked out the door.

I followed her to the door and saw her walk down the hall and out the front door of Fields Hall. Then I went over and sat down next to Rochester. "What do you think, boy? You like her?"

He scrambled to his feet and put his head in my lap. "Is that a yes? She's nice, isn't she? Why weren't you friendlier to her?"

He buried his nose in my crotch. "You are such a goof. Are you jealous?" I used the baby-voice I'd never been able to use with a human offspring. "Is the puppy jealous?"

I realized that I was sitting in my office talking baby-talk to a dog—not exactly the most professional behavior for a director of public relations and publicity. I scratched behind Rochester's ears once more, then returned to my desk. I thought it would be a good idea to take the photos from Barbara's application over to the biology department, as Lili had suggested, and see if a professor there could recognize anything.

The college website told me that Dr. Searcy was the senior professor who specialized in plant biology, and he had a class in Green Hall, the science building, which finished at three o'clock. Green Hall was probably the oldest classroom building on campus and the least "green" of any of our buildings. One of the main targets of the capital campaign was a new building for the physical sciences, with up-to-date computer-equipped labs.

Dr. Searcy was an older guy in a white lab coat, totally bald, standing at the front of the class talking to a student. I waited until he was finished, then walked up to him as he was packing his briefcase and introduced myself. "I was hoping you could take a look at some pictures I have," I said. "Help me figure out what kind of plants I'm looking at."

"You have them with you?"

I opened the booklet Barbara had created and handed it to him. "Pretty common plants," he said, flipping the pages. "You say these were taken here in Bucks County?"

"Up along the Tohickon Creek, I believe."

He nodded and hummed to himself. Then he stopped. "This one isn't local," he said, pointing to the Common Shooting Star."

"That's what I was wondering about. Could it be?"

He looked more closely at the photo. "The other plants in the background are all native to this area. There isn't any reason why it wouldn't be there—this is just far from its habitat."

"Somerset County," I said. "South of Pittsburgh, where Pennsylvania meets Maryland and West Virginia."

"Why exactly are you interested in these photos?" he asked, handing the booklet back to me.

"If this Common Shooting Star isn't normally found here in Bucks County, and some of them were found here, would that make them endangered?"

"You'd better come up to my office." He picked up his briefcase and I followed him into the dark, gloomy corridor, and up a set of broad marble stairs, worn down by a hundred years of students trudging to class and to faculty offices.

Dr. Searcy's office was stuffed to the gills with biology books, photos of plants, preserved samples in glass cases, and a host of other junk that made it difficult to move around inside. He navigated his way between a teetering pile of books in cardboard mailers and a life-sized stuffed bird. "Ruffed grouse?" I asked.

"You know your birds?"

"I grew up in Stewart's Crossing. Just down the river. We had to memorize all the state stuff in second grade—ruffed grouse, whitetail deer, brook trout, mountain laurel. Can't say that knowledge has come in handy until now."

He sat down at his computer and pulled up a website of endangered plants in the state of Pennsylvania. "Yes, there it is," he said. "Common Shooting Star. Endangered, with a limited habitat in Somerset County." He looked up at me. "Are you sure this photo was taken around here?"

"Not a hundred percent. But if it was, would it be a big deal?"

"To a biologist, certainly. To an environmentalist as well. " He sighed. "You know who would have been a good person to talk to? Joe Dagorian, in the admissions office. He was a very ardent amateur naturalist."

I shivered. "I found this booklet at his home. And I believe he was attempting to stop development in the area where the photos were taken."

"Then I believe you need to speak to the police, young man," he said, in what I was sure was his best teacher voice.

"I believe that too, sir," I said.

Listening to Reason

When I got back to my office, I called Tony Rinaldi and got his voice mail. I left him a message. I was ready to head for home when a meeting request popped up on my computer for the first thing the next morning. The note that accompanied it listed an agenda: Babson would talk about a potential trip to the West Coast; Sally was to talk about recruiting, Sam about exhibition games with prominent colleges, and Mike about donors. I was supposed to talk about press opportunities.

Rochester was nosing around my knees, eager to get a move on. "Sorry, pup, can't leave quite yet. Our fearless leader needs some work done."

He sighed deeply and settled next to my chair in a big golden heap. I scrambled to get ready, putting everything else aside, and by sixI had gotten a fix on the major media opportunities in San Francisco and Los Angeles. I wanted to drive up to the Tohickon Creek and see if I could find that Common Shooting Star—but it was already dark by the time Rochester and I left Fields Hall.

At home that night, after I had walked and fed Rochester, I was still restless. I prowled around the house looking for something to do to take my mind off thoughts of murder and dating—which both seemed about equally dangerous. There was a loose tread on the staircase, and the kitchen door needed new hinges. A big piece of molding had fallen off the front window and needed to be put back into place. There were a half-dozen other little things that needed to be done.

I found my father's old tool kit in the garage. Picking up a hammer I remembered him using, I thought of him. What would he have thought of how I'd ended up? He didn't like Mary, though he was always polite to her. He had been eager to have grandchildren, and for the first couple of years Mary and I were married he had asked me every time we spoke.

Then she had her first miscarriage, and he stopped asking. Occasionally he would talk about a friend and his

173

grandkids, and I could hear a tone of wistfulness in his voice. Would a granddog have satisfied him? He had never been much for animals when I was a kid. Somehow I couldn't imagine him driving around with a bumper sticker that read "Ask me about my son's golden retriever."

I fiddled around fixing things until I couldn't focus on the tools any more, then spent some time on the floor stroking Rochester's golden fur.

When I woke the next morning I thought about shooting up to Tohickon Creek on my way to work, but there was no time, by the time I walked Rochester, ate breakfast, showered and dressed. I made it up to campus just a couple of minutes before the meeting with Babson.

He was at his most imperial. He asked Sam to see if he could set up an exhibition game between our basketball team and a comparable team in California. "I'll look into it, President Babson," Sam said.

"I asked you to be prepared for this meeting," Babson said.

"I was at a game at Lehigh last night and didn't check my email until this morning," he said. "I will get on it today, though."

Babson demanded my media report next, and even though it was thrown together quickly he accepted it without much comment. He was more critical of Sally's report on high schools he should visit, though. "I wanted more than just a roster, I wanted an itinerary. How do I know which of these schools are close to each other or how many I can visit in a day?"

I had the feeling Sally was thinking on her feet. "I wanted to get some feedback from you, President Babson. How many schools do you think you could visit, if they were close together? Would you mind attending evening receptions? How much time will you have to spare from fund-raising events? If we had a fund-raiser and a candidate reception in the same hotel, could you go back and forth?" She asked half a dozen more questions and Babson backed down.

174

"Well, that'll take some time to work out. Let me think about it. Write me a memo."

Last of all he came to Mike for a report on the possible major donors who should get a personal visit. It was obvious that Mike had a staff at his disposal who could pull together a request like Babson's on a moment's notice. Mike had printouts of alumni organized by zip code, by class year and by office location. "We've got significant clusters in San Francisco, downtown Los Angeles, Hollywood, and Long Beach," Mike said. "I recommend three cocktail receptions and individual solicitation of these twelve major donors. " He had lists of whose employers matched employee gifts and records of past donations.

"This is the kind of research I like to see," Babson said. "This is professional, quality work."

"It's the only way we're going to make our total," Mike said. "We've each got to work as hard as we can."

I thought Mike was being pretty smarmy, but I held my tongue. I was sure he had more notice than the rest of us about the meeting, and I made a mental note to ask Dezhanne about it.

Luckily I ran into her on my way back to my office. "No, we just heard about the California thing late yesterday afternoon like you did," she said. "He sent someone to my Spanish class when it ended to drag me over to work, and he ordered us all pizza and made us stay until like nine o'clock. Everybody was going crazy. You know how he gets—like every little thing can set him off. Total roid rage, if you ask me."

"Roid rage?"

She lowered her voice. "I think he must be taking steroids. I mean, have you looked at his body?"

"Not my type," I said dryly.

"He's not mine either, believe me. But he's got muscles on muscles. You don't bulk up that way naturally. Roid rage is one of the side effects of steroid use—that and limp dick syndrome."

"Don't even go there," I said. Then I remembered the prescription I'd seen on Mike's desk for Viagra.

175

Those nasty side effects would explain his needing that drug.

Dezhanne juggled the folders she was carrying. "It would have been almost comical last night, if it hadn't been so scary. He was even making the Two J's work."

"The two jays?"

"Juan and Jose. These two idiots from the football team who are like his personal mascots. They're always hanging around the office, joking around with him in that dumb jock kind of way. I'll bet they're on roids, too."

I remembered Tony Rinaldi mentioning a problem with steroids on the campus. Could Dezhanne be right? Were Mike and his buddies involved in it somehow?

I found myself staring at Dezhanne's earlobes. In place of her standard disks, she wore these globes that looked like the Death Star from one of the *Star Wars* movies, with spikes sticking out all over. "Don't those hurt?" I asked.

"What?"

"Those things in your ears."

"Honestly, I don't even notice them," she said. "I've had these in for a couple of days. I've been so stressed out working for Mr. M." She lowered her voice. "Last night, he even said that he was glad that someone had killed Mr. Dagorian. That Mr. D had been a thorn in his side, keeping him from doing everything he wanted, and now the old fart was out of the way."

I raised my eyebrows at her.

"I swear, that's what he said. Sometimes the guy is just not for real. It was like, get out the whips and beat us until we produce. I don't know how much more I can take of it. Except that it's real good money."

"I can't offer you much encouragement," I said. "I have a feeling things are going to stay this bad until the campaign is over."

"Well, at least by then I'll have graduated and I'll be out of this place. I will graduate some day, won't I?"

"I did."

"Yeah, but you came back." She waved and walked off.

I turned around and instead of going back to my own office I went to Sally's. "You have a minute?" I asked, standing in her office door.

"Sure, come on in. These applications will still be here."

I closed the door behind me and sat down across from Sally. She looked tired, with dark circles under her eyes. Her hair was pulled back into a ponytail, and she wore her customary Fair Isle sweater.

"I was just talking to the work study student I share with Mike, and something she said jumped out at me. " I told her about Mike's problems with Joe.

"You don't think Mike could have killed Joe, do you?" she asked.

"The police always say they look for motive, opportunity, and means. Mike had the motive—Joe was always getting in his way, complaining about everything Mike tried to do. You must have seen that, too."

She nodded. "I can't remember a meeting when Joe and Mike didn't argue. But would you kill someone over that?"

"I'm sure Mike is under a lot of pressure to perform," I said. "You've seen the way Babson operates. Any of us could be fired if we don't provide the results he wants. That could really be stressing Mike out. " I pointed at the piles of paperwork around her. "Look at you—you're working hard, and you're stressed. What if Mike just broke?"

"At the launch party," she said. "He was under a huge amount of pressure that night."

"And we've both seen him go off on people. Suppose he argued with Joe again, and he just lost control."

"But what about the knife? Why would he be carrying the knife?"

"We know that Joe and Mike argued a couple of times that night. Suppose Mike just couldn't take it anymore, and decided it was time to end it with Joe once and for all. He picked up the knife and then stalked Joe until he was outside."

"Have you told this to that police officer?"

177

"Rinaldi? No. It just came to me, based on what Dezhanne said. I wanted to talk to you first."

"Well, I don't think you should say anything yet. You don't have any real evidence, after all. It's just a bunch of speculation and what if. And Mike's your boss. If he's innocent, and he finds out you talked to the police about him, you'll be fired so fast."

"But what if he's not?"

"If he's not, the police will figure it out. They look for evidence and stuff. Things that really prove something."

I sighed. "I guess you're right. " Even as I said it, though, I was thinking about how I could get some of that evidence Rinaldi would need.

"Steve. Look at me."

I looked at her. "If Mike killed Joe MacCormac, and you start nosing around, you're putting yourself in danger. You have to leave it up to the police."

I stood up. "I hear you. Listen, I'll let you get back to work. I need to do some thinking."

I walked slowly back to my office. As I passed Mike's, he saw me through the open door and motioned me in. "How's your research going?" he asked. "You find out anything yet?"

For a moment I was startled, and my pulse raced. Did he know I was talking about him? Then I remembered I was supposed to be working on alumni profiles for him. "I started," I said. "But then Babson sent us all off on this California thing."

"You have to learn how to work with him. He'll ask for something, then send you off in thirteen different directions, and then expect you to come up with that first thing he asked for. You need to narrow your focus."

It was like everything he said had a dual meaning. Narrow my focus? To him as the murderer?

"I've seen that police guy in and out of your office a few times," he said. "You've been spending a lot of time trying to solve Joe's murder, haven't you?"

"I've been trying to help out. You know it's not good PR for us to have an unsolved murder on our campus."

178

"Or for fund-raising either. But I'm worried that you're drawing too much attention to them by pursuing this. If I were you, I'd let the police do the work. You know, it's dangerous to play around in something like murder."

I couldn't figure out what Mike's game was, but I thought I'd play along. The adrenaline rushing through my veins made me bolder. "I know," I said. "But the police think the killer might be Ike Arumba, from the Rising Sons. I just don't believe he did it. I can't sit by and let him take the rap if he's innocent. The sooner we can get this resolved, the sooner we can all move on. Eastern College will survive this—it's gone through worse."

He stood up. He was bigger than I was, a couple of years younger and a lot stronger. I remembered that he had played football in college, and thought that was why those two football players, Juan and Jose, were always hanging around with him.

Or were they some kind of henchmen for him? Could they have helped him kill Joe? I backed toward the door of his office. It was lunchtime, and many people in the building had gone out. Was anyone close enough to hear me if I yelled for help?

"I'm the best fund-raiser this college has ever had. I could be at Harvard right now. And if I can carry off this capital campaign I will be. I'll be the best fund-raiser there is. I wouldn't let a two-bit admissions director stop me, or interfere with my plans. No one can tell me how to run my office. I know what I'm doing. I'm in control."

I backed away a little more, very slowly. I remembered those angry emails he had sent to Joe, that Rinaldi had mentioned? Was there really a motive there?

I was thinking fast, but I was very aware of everything around me. I scanned the office for things to throw at Mike, to knock him down or stun him so he couldn't chase me as I ran down the hall toward the front door of Fields Hall.

"Joe thought he was so important," Mike continued. "Just because he'd been at Eastern since Jesus wore short pants. He thought he could run this college. He

179

took away my telethon volunteers to recruit high school students. He wanted to have me fired. Hah! Can you imagine that! Every time I made a suggestion, Joe criticized me. All he cared about was his obscure scholarship funds. For a Nebraska high school student who intends to major in English. For a child of Ukrainian immigrants who wishes to study United States history. You know the kind of silly, Mickey Mouse funds he liked to set up."

I felt like Scheherazade in the *Tales of the Arabian Nights*, talking to save my own life. I wondered how to divert Mike's attention, to stall him until someone else showed up. "Joe was pretty set in his ways. You must have argued with him a lot."

"I'll be frank with you Steve, because I know it'll go no further. This is the slowest time for a campaign, after the nucleus fund has been collected and the first surge of pledges have been paid in. Everybody gives at the beginning, and then at the end we make a big pitch to get over the top, but during the middle it's slow. I can't afford to distract my attention or my staff's attention. That's the only way we'll ever succeed."

"And when Eastern succeeds, you'll be the hero," I said.

"I'll be hot when this campaign is over, Steve. I'll be the best fund-raiser around if I can carry this campaign off. Imagine, five hundred million dollars for a dinky little college like Eastern. I can go anywhere, do anything I want when this is over. I'll be able to write my own ticket. I'm not going to let anybody stand in my way. And that means I need you to back off talking to the police. Let this thing die down of its own accord."

Let it die down because you don't want to get caught, I thought. "I can't do that," I said.

"I was afraid you wouldn't listen to reason," Mike said. "You don't want me to take the next step."

Mike's right hand pulled quickly out of the pocket of his sports jacket, and I saw the glint of metal. I jumped back, banging against the door frame. I thought my heart was going to beat its way out of my chest.

Then I realized Mike was holding a cell phone. "You don't want me to call President Babson and have him tell you to back off."

He looked at me strangely. He must have seen the fear in my face. "What, did you think I was going to knife you or something?"

I nodded.

"Jesus. " He sat back down in his chair. "Are you telling me you think I killed Joe?"

I was having trouble catching my breath, but I managed to say, "You had a motive."

"Steve. You've been watching too many cop shows on TV. Sure, Joe was stonewalling me at every opportunity. But I'm a lot smarter than he ever was. I anticipated everything he tried to do and blocked him. He could have stayed alive for years and it wouldn't have bothered my plans one bit."

His desk phone began to ring. "And there's another thing. I think you have to be a little off balance to go so far as to kill someone. And I know exactly where I'm putting every footstep I take."

He picked up his phone and I took that opportunity to duck out of his office.

Playing Hooky

When I got back to my office Rochester was all over me. It was like he smelled the leftover fear on me. I spent a couple of minutes just petting him and thinking. I still wasn't sure Mike MacCormac hadn't killed Joe—but I recognized that I didn't have any evidence against him and I didn't want to look like a fool pushing Rinaldi. And if the same person had killed Perpetua Kaufman, then I didn't know how Mike could have a motive against her.

I realized that I still hadn't told Tony about the photos from Barbara Seville's portfolio. I dialed the Leighville police station and sat on hold for a minute while he came to the phone.

"If you're calling with more support for Ike Arumba, you can give it up," he said. "I checked the timetable and there's no way he could have killed Dagorian and still made it up to the stage to sing."

"That's good to hear," I said. "But I was calling about something else. Maybe you'll think this is weird but it kind of fits. " I told him about finding Barbara's photographs at Joe's house, and the connection between the Bucks County Nature Conservancy and Bar-Lyn Investments. "Both Joe and Perpetua were involved in trying to stop Bar-Lyn from building."

I could hear him taking notes. "I'll look into it," he said.

I hung up feeling a little better, though I still didn't feel like working. I forced myself to go back to the personality profiles for Mike, because he had asked for them twice by then, and I didn't want to be empty-handed when he asked again.

By three o'clock I was dead bored, flipping through my email searching for a distraction. Babson had sent a message detailing revisions to the college budget. It was written in bureaucratic jargon, the kind of language I was seeking to eliminate in representing the college, but it boiled down to more money for Mike's fundraising efforts and less in the pot for the rest of us. I reflected for a couple of minutes about how Mike's single-mindedness seemed to be working, and I was depressed to realize that I could never be that way.

"Knock, knock," Lili said from my doorway. Rochester looked up at her, then put his head back down.

"Hey, come on in." I motioned her to the chair next to my desk.

She was dressed in jeans and a thick Icelandic sweater, with a colorful wool scarf, and her curly hair was pulled back from her face. She had a messenger bag slung sideways around her neck. "I'm bored," she said. "I need to get away. I was hoping I could convince you to play hooky with me. We could drive out and see that property where the pictures were taken."

"An inspired idea. I need to get out of here, too."

From the Bucks County Nature Conservancy site, and a mapping program, I pulled up directions to the property Bar-Lyn Investments owned.

I stood up. "Come on, Rochester, let's go for a walk." I stretched his expandable leash a couple of times, expecting him to jump up and go in to his deranged kangaroo routine, but instead he stayed in place.

"He's usually much friendlier." I pulled on my coat, scarf, and hat, and reached down to hook up Rochester's leash. He turned away from me, trying to hide his head.

"No nonsense, dog." I reached around his downy neck and hooked the leash, but he decided to play dead. I tugged on the leash, to no avail. "I'll drag you out of here if I have to."

Lili was giggling. "Here, let me try." She held her hand out and I handed her the leash. Immediately, Rochester leapt up, then tackled her.

"Rochester!" I said.

"It's all right," she said, reaching down to scratch behind his ears. "Are you a good boy?"

"No," I said, as he woofed and nodded his head.

She let him have his head as we walked out of Fields Hall. "Want to take my car?" I asked. "You can navigate."

I opened the back door of the BMW and Rochester looked at me like I was crazy. "He usually sits up front with me," I said. I tugged the leash again, and he jumped up onto the back seat.

We drove up along the River Road to Point Pleasant, then turned inland on Tohickon Hill Road, taking a couple of turns on small lanes that skirted woods and farmland. "That must be it," Lili said, pointing ahead, to where a large sign proclaimed that it was the future site of Tohickon Creek Adult Living, a project of Bar-Lyn Development.

I parked at a wide space in the road and Lili and I climbed out. I opened the back door and Rochester scrambled out, immediately sniffing a bush and peeing. Lili pulled a very expensive-looking camera from her messenger bag and hung it around her neck.

The photos Barbara had taken were next to a piece of water, so we walked the property looking for the creek or one of its tributaries. It was chilly but bracing, not really freezing, and there was still enough sun to warm the open spaces. While Rochester romped and sniffed, Lili and I walked along the water, looking for the Common Shooting Star.

"It's too early for it to be blossoming, but we should be able to recognize it by its foliage," she said. She stopped periodically to take pictures—a couple of me, a couple of Rochester, some of the landscape.

"I needed this," she said. "I was going stir crazy in my office."

"I'm glad you came by. I've been stewing about Joe's murder too much. " I told her about my confrontation with Mike MacCormac.

"You're not too bright, are you?" she asked, stepping up close to me. "You shouldn't go around confronting people you think are murderers."

"Really? Why not?"

"Your dog loves you. You wouldn't want him to be all alone, would you?"

She was so close then. The chill seemed to highlight the scent of her floral perfume, and I leaned forward and kissed her again.

"Mm," she said. She kissed me back. "And see, if someone killed you, you'd miss this, too."

I wrapped my arms around her heavy sweater and pulled her close. We kissed again, standing in the clearing, and then Rochester started barking.

I pulled away from Lili long enough to say, "Rochester! Quiet!"

He didn't shut up, and she stepped back. "Maybe he found something."

I cursed the damned dog under my breath as I followed Lili to where Rochester was standing, by the bank of the creek, barking at something.

"It's probably a squirrel or something," I said.

He stopped barking as we approached, looking from me to Lili and back.

"I think he found the plant," she said. "Look, don't the leaves match?" She chucked Rochester under the neck, and he stretched his head back to give her easier access.

I held the photo up and we compared it to the plant. There were no flowers, but the stem and leaves seemed to match. Lili took a bunch of pictures.

We were just finishing when a man's voice boomed out behind us. "This is private property, and you're trespassing."

We looked up at a tall, bald man in a camel-hair coat. Rochester began barking at him.

"Rochester. Shh," I said.

"What are you doing with my daughter's photo album?" the man asked. "Who are you?"

"You're Barbara's father, aren't you?" I asked. "My name is Steve Levitan. I just took over the technical writing class she's in." I nodded toward Lili. "This is Dr. Weinstock, from the Fine Arts Department. I thought Barbara's photos were so well-done that I showed them to Dr. Weinstock."

"Your daughter has real talent," Lili said. "I'd like her to take my photography course."

"You shouldn't be out here," Seville said. "You aren't part of that group of nature freaks, are you?"

"The Bucks County Nature Conservancy?" I asked.

185

"That's the one. You're here to keep screwing up my project, aren't you?"

"Not at all." I took Lili's hand. "We just thought we'd come out to see the place where Barbara took her photos. We'll go now."

"You took over Barbara's class. So you must have known her other teacher. Stupid old ex-nun."

"Professor Kaufman? No, I didn't know her. The department chair just needed a replacement quickly." I started backing away from him.

"Not so fast." He pulled a handgun from his coat pocket. "I know you. Barbara has been talking about you. You've been snooping into her professor's murder."

I thought the best defense was to play innocent. "Professor Kaufman? I thought she died from a faulty space heater."

"Don't try and fool me. You know exactly what happened to her, and to that jerk from the admissions office, and why. And you know what that means, don't you?"

Lili looked at me and squeezed my hand. I could see Rochester tensed behind Seville. "I don't know anything you're talking about," I said.

"It means I can't let either of you leave here. " He raised his hand and aimed at Lili.

Surprises

Lili was fearless. She raised her camera to her eye and started snapping shots of Seville aiming at us. Rochester lunged at Seville from behind, and as he squeezed the trigger, the dog knocked him to the ground, so the bullet went wide. Seville dropped the gun as he fell, and it landed a few feet away.

Rochester was on top of Seville on the ground, the big man struggling to push the dog off him. "Give me your scarf," I said to Lili. "And then call 911."

She pulled her scarf off and I joined Rochester, kneeling on Seville's back. I tied Lili's scarf around his hands, behind his back, as she picked up his gun. Then she pulled her cell phone from her pocket and dialed.

"Tell them to send Sergeant Rinaldi," I said.

Seville continued to struggle, but with me sitting on his butt, and Rochester at alert next to his head, he wasn't going anywhere.

"You sure know how to show a girl a good time," Lili said.

"You were amazing. You aren't afraid of anything, are you?"

"Spiders. Being stranded somewhere without a book to read. Getting a degenerative disease so that I become a prisoner inside my body. And a few more things, too."

"But not men with guns."

"I spent three months in Beirut as a photojournalist during the last civil war. I learned my camera can be a weapon, too. Once I knew that, I could face down anything."

Seville tried again to push me off his back, but I sat fast. "Amazing. Beirut? Really?"

She nodded. "I did some freelancing for the Miami *Herald*. I was traveling with a reporter up to Hamra when we were stopped at a security checkpoint. They took away our passports and all our ID, confiscated the van we were driving in and took away our translator and our driver. They tried to take my cameras but I kneed the guy in the balls and he backed away."

"See?" I said to Seville. "You got away lucky."

"You'll regret this," he said, his head resting against the sparse winter grass. "I'm going to see you both behind bars."

"There will be bars between us, but you'll be on the wrong side of them," I said. "I looked up at Lili. "So what happened?"

"They kept us in this dark room for two days. Only fed us a little water and some mushy rice. Finally our translator got word to someone in his family, who contacted the embassy, who sent someone out to get us. It was scary but it was also incredibly tedious."

Seville gave up struggling and wouldn't say anything further. It took nearly ten minutes for the first cop car to arrive. By then I had called Tony Rinaldi on his cell and explained to him where we were and what we were doing. He made contact with the patrol car, so the officer had already been briefed by the time he approached us across the open space.

He cuffed Seville and stood him up. "These people are trespassers and they attacked me!" he sputtered to the cop. "I demand that you let me go and arrest them."

"Let's go wait in the car until the sergeant gets here," the cop said. "I suggest you folks warm up, too."

I was shivering, and my pants were damp with the last snow from the ground. I was grateful to stretch my arms and legs and then walk to the BMW. Rochester jumped into the back seat without complaint, and Lili and I sat in front with the heater going.

"I'm sorry to have dragged you into this," I said. "I never would have brought you out here if I'd thought we could get into trouble."

"Sometimes I complain that the life of a college professor is boring and routine," she said. "I won't be saying that for a while."

Rochester snored lightly on the back seat. I plugged my iPhone into the adapter for the radio and asked Lili, "Any kind of music you prefer?"

"Let me see what you've got. " Our fingers touched as I handed her the phone. We listened to some country music for a while, then a couple of show tunes, until Tony Rinaldi arrived.

He came over to talk to us first, and we both got out of the car, leaving Rochester in the back seat. I explained everything that had happened. Then he went to talk to Richard Seville. After a long time, he came back to us. "Let's recap," he said. "You were trespassing, and Mr. Seville confronted you. You argued, and he felt he had to pull his gun to defend himself."

"Excuse me?" I asked. "Is that what he says?"

"He is the property owner."

"There are no posted signs," Lili said. "Not a single no trespassing sign. So he can't pull that nonsense."

Tony nodded. "I agree. Which leaves us with things the other way around. He shot at you, and you were defending yourselves against him. Since he's the one with the gun, I'm likely to believe you. But unless you're willing to press charges I can't take him in."

"I'll do it," I said. "But what about arresting him for killing Joe Dagorian and Perpetua Kaufman? He almost admitted it to us."

"Almost admitting is like almost pregnant," Tony said. "You don't get a result in either case. But I've been doing some investigating myself. You know, that is my job."

"Yes, I know." Rochester forced his way into the front seat and looked through the driver's side window at us. He barked once. I just looked over at him.

"I'm close to putting a case together against Seville," Tony continued. "I can hold him on the assault charge until we get a judge and a bail hearing. And by then I hope to have a lot more to hold against him. I'll work with Rick Stemper on charging him with both murders."

While Tony and I were talking, Lili pulled a netbook out of her messenger bag and uploaded the pictures from her camera to it. "Give me your email address," she said to Tony. "As soon as I can get a wi-fi signal I'll email the pictures I took to you."

189

Tony gave it to her. I had to promise to meet him at the Leighville Police Station the next morning to give a formal statement. He took custody of the book of Barbara's photos, and let us go.

"I'll drive you back to campus," I said, turning on the car.

"We don't have to head back so quickly," she said. "You know anyplace around here where we could get something to eat?"

I thought of More than Chocolate, Gail's café in Stewart's Crossing. "You like chocolate?"

"You bet."

Rochester went to sleep in the back seat, and I drove us down to Stewart's Crossing. While we waited for our food, Lili opened her netbook and did some quick tweaking on the photos, then emailed them to Tony.

After a very nice dinner, I mentioned that we were so close to my townhouse, and asked if Lili might like to see it. I thought I was being very suave, but she saw right through me. "Only if the tour includes the bedroom," she said.

"I can manage that," I said, though I wasn't a hundred percent sure I could. After all, it had been a long time.

We got back to the house, and Rochester went right to his bed in the kitchen and settled down. I guess he figured he'd earned a good long nap, and I agreed.

Lili and I went upstairs, and I did manage, well enough to satisfy us both. After we cuddled and dozed for a while, I drove her back up to the campus. Rochester chose to come along as our chaperon.

"It's been a hell of a second date," she said, as we pulled up next to her car in the faculty parking lot.

"In a good way, I hope."

"A very good way. " She leaned across and kissed my cheek. "Can't wait to see what you've got lined up for date number three."

I drove back downriver to Stewart's Crossing, where I took Rochester for a long walk around River Bend, feeling very satisfied with myself. It's not every day a

190

man faces down death, catches a killer, and makes love to a beautiful woman, after all.

The next morning Rochester decided to take the day off and stay home. I figured he'd earned it. Instead of driving up the hill to the college, I stopped at the police station. Tony had worked most of the night, gathering evidence against Richard Seville, and the district attorney was preparing an indictment against him for the murders of Joe Dagorian and Perpetua Kaufman. I gave Tony a full statement of everything I knew, interspersed with a lot of questions.

He must have said, "I can't put that in my report," every time I mentioned something Rochester had done, though.

"You and your dog seem to have a knack for getting into trouble," he said. "And if my chief ever figures out a dog is out-thinking me, then my job is on the line."

"No worries. I think he and I have a woman to keep us out of trouble for a while."

"You and the photographer? You could do a lot worse. She's beautiful—and those pictures she took while Seville had the gun on you both? Amazing."

"Yeah, the rest of the evening was pretty amazing, too."

He raised his eyebrows but didn't say anything more. "Keep in touch," he said. "I'm sure we'll need more from you as the DA puts the case together."

He opened the drawer of his desk and pulled out a bag of rawhide bones. "For the dog," he said.

"Thanks. You ever need him to consult on a case, you just let me know."

Second Chances

The sun came out, and I drove up to Eastern with my windows cracked open. I knew that spring was still at least a month away, but a boy can hope. I had barely got my coat off in my office when Ike Arumba came to my door.

"I really want to thank you for what you did, Mr. Levitan," he said. "The police have dropped all the charges against me, and Sally hired me to start working part-time at the admissions office. It means I'll have to give up the Rising Sons, but there's a freshman baritone who can take my place."

"Congratulations, Ike. Remember Sally is giving you a second chance and you can't make any more mistakes."

"I've learned my lesson. I'm excited about getting back to work. Fortunately my course load is light this term and I can really get into it. Sally says I can apply for the assistant director's job, too."

"Well, good luck."

Next in my office was President Babson. "I understand the police have someone in custody for Joe's murder? And Perpetua Kaufman was murdered as well? It wasn't just an accident with her space heater?"

I filled him in. "I think we're going to need a press release. Shall I draft one?"

"Please. It's sad, losing Joe, and Perpetua. I knew her for years, you know. And all for something so silly as a plant. " He shook his head. "Let me know if you think I should address the press directly."

"Will do. I'll have the release for you shortly."

I spent a while on the release, aiming for the right tone, trying to downplay Eastern's role in the whole scenario. When I had gone over it so many times the words were swimming on the page, I gave up and emailed it to Babson for his approval. Then I went down to Sally's office. "I understand you're getting some more help around here."

"Ike starts Monday, and I can feel the relief already," she said. "I can see light at the end of the tunnel. Of course, the light is still a long way off."

"And remember, sometimes the light at the end of the tunnel is just an oncoming train," I said.

She made shooing motions. "Go. I have work to do. " As I was walking back to my office, I ran into Lou Segusi, from my tech writing class, in the hallway. I remembered I had promised to talk to him about his career prospects.

"So you want to be a technical writer?" I asked.

"I've got bigger problems. " He slumped down in the chair across from my desk. "I'm in, like, huge trouble, and I can't figure out what to do. You've been really nice and I was hoping maybe you could give me some advice."

Rochester got up from his place by the French doors and walked over to Lou, sniffing him. Lou dropped his good left arm down and stroked the dog's head, and Rochester sat down next to him.

"Is this about all the papers you've been writing?" I asked. "They aren't all for you, are they?"

He shook his head. "It started last year. I can speed-read, and write really fast, so I was always finished with my papers super early, then just hanging around the dorm playing games and shit. One of my roommates asked me if I could write a paper for him. It was on *Wuthering Heights*, which I read in high school, so I was like, no problem, dude. It was just something to keep busy."

"And against the college's Honor Code and plagiarism policy."

"Yeah, I know. But it seemed like no big deal at the time. Then he told a friend, and I wrote a paper for him. And before you know it, I had these guys lined up for me to write papers. Mostly guys from the football team, but eventually their girlfriends and their roommates and all. I made good money, and it was really interesting, you know? It was like taking all these extra courses. I looked at it like I was learning a lot myself, and getting paid for it to boot. That's when I started to think about

193

getting a job after graduation as a technical writer. You know, like, getting paid legit."

As a teacher, the whole idea of what Lou had been doing was anathema. But as a smart guy who could write quickly myself, I could see his point. "So what happened? You broke your arm and you couldn't meet deadlines?"

"More like my arm got broken for me," he said, frowning.

"Someone broke your arm? Someone who got a bad grade on a paper you wrote?"

"I never got a bad grade for anybody I wrote for. This was different."

I sat back in my chair, waiting for him to go on. "I had this crush on this girl. Desiree DiLiberti. Only she had a boyfriend, one of the guys from the football team. So I figured I would just give up. Then she came to me and asked me to write a paper for her."

"Yes?"

"And we, kind of, you know, started fooling around in her dorm room."

"In place of her paying you?"

"No! Not at all. I never even thought of that. I just thought, like, cool, she's into me, too."

"Let me guess. The boyfriend came in."

"With one of his buddies. The two of them are always together. I swear, if it wasn't for Desiree I'd think the two dudes were into each other."

"Jose and Juan?"

"You know them?"

I nodded. "They do some work for the director of alumni relations."

He slumped back in his seat, pulling his hand back from Rochester, who looked up and started sniffing Lou's leg. "I am so screwed."

"Who broke your arm?"

"Juan. Desiree is his girlfriend. Jose held me down so Juan could do it."

"That's criminal assault," I said. "You need to report that to the police."

194

"But then they'd say how I was writing papers for them and their buddies, and I'd get kicked out of school."

"I don't think they'd finger you, because they would, too. They violated the honor code just as much as you did. Even more, because they did something criminal, too."

"But they're football players. And like you said, they're tight with the guy in the alumni office, too. He'll protect them."

I could see his dilemma. Even at Eastern, which prided itself on academics, there was a double standard when it came to student-athletes. Professors were routinely asked to excuse students from class, or assignments, so that they could attend practice or away games. Jocks got extra tutoring to help them keep their grades up, and at many colleges they were pampered with all kinds of perks.

Just like with Ike, I could relate to his problem in a personal way. I'd done some things I didn't think were big deals, which ended up getting me in a lot of trouble. And I'd had a lot of trouble bouncing back. How much tougher would it be for Lou, if he were kicked out of Eastern in his last semester? He wouldn't have the degrees or work experience I had to fall back on.

What was I turning into? The Mother Teresa of distressed students? I sighed.

Rochester gave up on being petted and went back to slump next to the French doors. I remembered Thomas Taylor, the homeless man who had been denied admission to Eastern, and how his life had fallen apart after that. The parallel wasn't exact, because obviously there was more wrong with Taylor than just disappointment. But it was another example of how a life could go off the rails based on one decision.

"All right," I said, leaning forward. "So far this has all been background. What's your current problem, and how do we get that taken care of?"

"You'll help me?"

"If you tell me what you need."

He wasn't taking on any new assignments or clients, he said. "I'm done with all that. It's just too much trouble. But Juan and Jose, they say I have to keep writing for them until I graduate, or they'll keep breaking other parts of my body."

"The way I see it, you've got two problems: criminal and academic. These guys have assaulted you and threatened you. That's a criminal matter. The ghostwriting and the violations of the honor code, that's academic. But they're both tied together."

"But I don't want to rat out all my clients, and if I tell anybody from the college about the papers they'll want to know who I wrote for."

I sat back in my chair. "You write well, Lou. That's a skill, and you could use that to help other students. Suppose I could negotiate a deal for you—you'd volunteer a certain number of hours in the writing lab, tutoring other students, until you graduate."

"I could do that," he said.

"There would have to be some kind of academic sanction as well. I don't know what that would be, but something short of expelling you, for sure. You can't fail any classes, because you've done all your own work. It wouldn't make sense to put you on academic probation, because you're about to graduate. And I can't see making you stand at a blackboard and write 'I will not write other students' papers' a thousand times."

I sighed. "Let me think about it, all right?"

"And what do I do about Jose and Juan?"

"I don't know, Lou. I'm making this up as I go. Just try and stay away from them for a couple of days."

"Not easy. We all live in Birthday House."

Birthday House was one of Eastern's largest dorms, donated by an alumnus named Hoare on his birthday years before—giving the college the opportunity to avoid having a dorm named Hoare House.

I scribbled my cell phone number on a piece of paper and handed it to Lou. "If you run into trouble, call me," I said.

He stood up, and he looked like the weight of the world had been lifted from his shoulders. "Thanks, Mr. Levitan. I really appreciate this. You're a lifesaver."

As he walked out, Santiago Santos passed him. "Good to know you're making an impact on young people," he said.

Rochester looked up, then slumped back to the floor. Santos didn't interest him.

I wondered how much Santos had heard of our conversation. I was sure he wouldn't approve of my hanging around with a student who flaunted college rules, or conspiring with the kid to avoid punishment. "I'm teaching a class again," I said. "A couple of days after I saw you last, the chair of the English department asked me to take over for an adjunct professor who passed away suddenly."

"Sudden death has a way of following you around. " He pulled out his laptop, put it on my desk, then sat down across from me and turned it on. "How does your boss feel about you teaching?"

"He's pleased I'm doing a favor for the English department."

He clicked a few keys on the laptop, obviously opening his file on me, then began typing some notes. "I want to make sure you're not over-extending yourself, Steve," he said. "You know how hard it is to come by good full-time jobs with benefits in this economy. And you know you need to impress your boss, so that he'll keep you on after this semester is over. I don't want to see you do anything that can screw this gig up."

"I'm not worried," I said, though of course I was. Every time I saw that paycheck automatically deposited into my bank account, every time I could pay the maintenance fees for River Bend, my electric and phone bills and credit card charges without sweating, I took a deep breath and said thank you to the gods of employment. I knew how easily I could lose everything that mattered to me, because I'd already been through that.

"How are you doing being around computers so much?"

I knew he was only looking out for me—but I was starting to get fed up. "Listen, Santiago, I'm forty-three years old. I made one mistake, and I paid for it. I'm still paying for it. I lost my job, my house and my wife. I know what's at stake here and I'm getting tired of you assuming I'm some slacker who doesn't think through his actions."

Even as I said it, I realized I was guilty of that—not thinking things through clearly enough. But I was damned if I was going to admit that.

To his credit, he didn't rise to the bait. I guess he was accustomed to parolees going off on him. He stayed calm, asking me questions about what I did every day, about how closely Mike MacCormac supervised me, and so on.

I felt like I'd rather have my eyeballs scratched out than answer the same questions over and over again, but I took some deep breaths and tried to stay calm and pleasant. Then my cell phone buzzed with an incoming text message.

"Excuse me for a minute," I said, pulling the phone to me and punching in my code. "Need yr help ASAP," the message read. "J&J locked me in closet in their room in BH."

"Shit. " I stood up. "That kid who was just here? He's in trouble. I've got to run over to the dorms."

"We're not finished yet, Steve."

I handed him the phone, then grabbed my coat and Rochester's leash. "That look like it can wait to you?" I asked. The dog jumped up and came over to me.

"You're not a security guard, Steve. Call the police."

I took the phone back from him. "I'm calling campus security," I said, hooking up Rochester's leash.

"Steve."

"Can't stay. Gotta dash. " Rochester was already straining at his leash, so we ducked through the French doors and out into the cold.

We hurried down the slope toward Birthday House, and I dialed the number for campus security and explained the problem. The operator said that she'd have an officer meet me in the lobby of the dorm.

As if he knew time was of the essence, Rochester loped down the hill, tugging me behind him, not bothering to stop and sniff or pee. I was out of breath by the time we reached the dorm, where a student assistant sat behind a wooden desk. Behind her were cubbyholes for packages, and stacks of forms for various purposes.

I pulled my ID out of my wallet. "I need a student room number. Jose Canusi and Juan Tanamera."

"Those guys," she said. "135. Down the hall to the right."

"When security shows up, send them down there."

Rochester led the way down the hall, the girl behind me calling, "Hey, that dog can't come in here."

We got to room 135 and I knocked on the door. No answer.

Fortunately, Eastern hadn't upgraded the locks on dorm room doors since I was a student. I pulled an old credit card out of my wallet and slid it between the door and the jamb. It took some wiggling, but eventually I felt the bolt slip and the door swung open.

Rochester pushed forward into the room. I dropped his leash and hurried over to the closet. Lou Segusi was slumped on the floor inside it, a piece of duct tape over his mouth. His good wrist had been bound behind his back with a belt, but he'd managed to use the fingers of his broken arm to text me.

As I knelt to pull the tape off, I heard two voices coming from down the hall, and a moment later one of them said, "What the hell is going on here?"

I looked around to see Juan and Jose in the doorway to the room.

Junior G-Man

I pulled the tape off Lou's mouth and stood up. "What did you guys think you were playing at here?" I demanded, in my best teacher voice.

"We found a rat," Jose said. Both wore their Eastern football jackets. And both of them were bigger than I was, with the added advantage of youth and training in physical combat

"And now we found another one," Juan said.

Rochester had nosed open a drawer on one of the desks, and began digging furiously inside it.

"Hey, make that dog stop that!" Jose said.

"What's going on in here?"

All four of us turned around to see a security guard in the doorway, a midddle-aged guy in a modified police uniform with the Eastern logo on the breast. "I had reason to believe that a student was being held against his will inside this room," I said, pointing to where Lou still sat on the floor in the closet.

Rochester grabbed a plastic bag full of pink tablets in his mouth and held it up. "Hey, that's mine," Jose said. "Give it back."

He reached over to take the bag from the dog, and Rochester growled at him through clenched teeth. Jose jumped back.

"This is crazy," Juan said. "All you guys need to get out of our room."

I flipped out my cell phone and hit the speed dial for Tony Rinaldi. "I think it's time for you to talk to the police," I said.

Juan lunged at me, trying to take the phone from my hand. Rochester rushed at him, still clenching the baggie in his jaws, and Juan stepped back. "I need your help up on campus," I said to Tony as soon as he answered. "ASAP. Birthday House dorm."

"What's up?"

"Can't talk," I said, as Rochester barked up a couple of times.

200

"Jesus, I hear the dog," Tony said. "I'll be up as soon as I can."

"We have a protocol for contacting the local police," the security guard began. Suddenly everyone was arguing at once—Lou accusing Juan and Jose, the two of them alternately protesting and trying to get the baggie back from Rochester, the guard trying to get everyone to just shut and listen to him. Somewhere in there I helped Lou stand up, and untied his left arm from behind his back. Rochester dropped the baggie he was holding, but lay down on the carpet with the baggie protected between his paws.

It took Tony Rinaldi to restore order. "Everybody shut up," he said, from the doorway. With the two hulking football players, Lou, me, Rochester and the security guard, the room was pretty crowded. It was a good thing they gave football players the most spacious dorm rooms.

"Steve. You first."

I told him about the text message from Lou, and how I had discovered him on the floor in the closet.

"How'd you get in there?" he asked Lou, who stood with his back against the wall, next to the closet door.

"I was walking back to my room after talking to Mr. Levilan when I saw Juan and Jose," he said. "I told them I wasn't going to write papers for them any more and they got really mad. They grabbed me and frog-marched me down here. Juan put that duct tape over my mouth while Jose tied my arm behind my back."

He flexed his left hand and arm. "It's the way they work. Jose is the one who held me down while Juan broke my arm."

"How did you get the cast on if they broke your arm?" Rinaldi asked.

"They did it the other day. After they caught me kissing Desiree."

Tony shook his head. "This just gets more and more complicated. I think we all need to go down to the station and work this out."

He called for a couple of uniformed cops to help with the transport. Then Rochester barked once. "What's up, boy?" I asked.

He stood up and picked up the baggie in his mouth, and walked it over to Tony, dropping it at Tony's feet. "These are steroids," Tony said, picking them up. I saw the pink tablets were thick and five-sided. "Where did he get these?"

"That drawer over there," I said. "Juan indicated in front of all of us that they belonged to him."

"It wasn't enough that you caught a murderer yesterday? You had to get me a break in my steroid case, too? My cup runneth over thanks to you, Steve. And I'm not liking it."

"Oh, sure," I said. "Thank me. Be gracious about it."

Juan and Jose started arguing again as the uniformed officers cuffed them and led them away. I walked Rochester back out to the lobby, where the girl on duty reminded me once again that dogs weren't allowed in the dorms.

"Got it," I said, waving my hand. "Thanks."

I took Rochester back up to my office, then drove down the hill to Leighville. As I was pulling into the police station parking lot, my cell rang. I saw from the display that it was Lili.

"Do you like eggplant parmigiana?" she asked.

"Love it. Used to make it all the time when I was young and broke. You want to go out to dinner somewhere?"

"I thought I'd cook for you. If that doesn't scare you away we'll see where we go from here."

"Men with guns? Scary. Women who can cook? Not scary at all."

"We'll see about that. You have Rochester with you today?"

"He's holding down the fort back at the office. I'm just about to go into the police station in Leighville."

"You need to give another statement?"

"Different case. " I gave her a quick rundown of Lou's problems and the steroid bust.

202

"You really are a junior G-man, aren't you?" she asked. "I can see my life getting a lot more interesting. Anyway, bring the dog. I think I can rustle up some hamburger for him, if that's OK."

"He'll love you." It felt funny, using the L word, even like that, when I hardly knew Lili. But I had a feeling we'd be getting to know each other better. I was glad she was willing to take Rochester in, too.

She gave me her address and we made plans to meet at six. Then I walked into the the station, where Tony was taking a statement from the security guard. I waited until he came out to the visitor area with the guard.

"Everything come together with Seville?" I asked, as the guard left and we walked down the hall to an interview room.

He nodded. "I just might get some sleep tonight. Seville's in custody. " He ushered me into the room, and we sat down across from each other at a scarred metal table. "Now let's talk about steroids and your friend Mr. Segusi."

I told him the whole story, beginning with hearing about Perpetua Kaufman's death from Lucas Roosevelt, and being asked to take over the class.

"How'd you know the kid was doing work for other students?" Tony asked.

"I didn't know for sure. But it was suspicious the way he always had papers to write, and on all different topics."

"I'm going to interview him next," Tony said.

I gave him Dezhanne's name. "She might be able to give you some more information on steroid use on campus," I said. "She seemed to know something about it."

I hesitated. I wanted to tell him about Mike MacCormac, but I was worried. If Mike was dealing drugs to college kids, then he'd get fired, and the capital campaign would get in trouble, and I might even lose my job, if Babson shut everything down. But I couldn't keep my mouth shut.

"You should talk to Mike MacCormac, too." I told Tony how I had begun working for Mike in January, mentioning his occasional rages, the way Juan and Jose were always hanging around his office, and the prescription for Viagra I'd found.

He took copious notes. "I take back what I said about getting home tonight," he said.

"Too bad for you. I have a double date tonight – with a dog and with a doll."

"Enjoy. " He handed me a bandana for Rochester with the Leighville police emblem on it, and a badge that named me as an honorary member of the Leighville police force.

"So I can show this when I get speeding tickets?"

"Get too many tickets and we'll take it away."

I picked up Rochester and we found our way to Lili's house. She and I had a great dinner, and he was delighted with the hamburger she'd prepared for him. Late that night we took Rochester for a walk around her neighborhood. "You lead a busy life," Lili said.

"Not really. Usually it's just me and the dog."

She put her gloved hand in mine. "You like it that way?"

"Sometimes. He's good company, but he's not a great conversationalist."

She laughed. "I can see you and I will have a lot to talk about."

I leaned over and kissed her. Her lips were cold, but they warmed up quickly. Then Rochester sniffed something and tugged so hard on his leash that he jerked my head away from Lili's. "Come on, Rochester wants to go home," she said. "And so do I."

***

Things settled back to normal at Eastern, though with one big difference: the team of Steve and Rochester added a new member, and the three of us spent a lot of time together, going to photography exhibits, enjoying home-cooked dinners, and watching movies on my new big-screen TV.

Richard Seville was arraigned for the murders of Joe Dagorian and Perpetua Kaufman. I didn't mention the case, or my part in it, to Barbara when I saw her in the technical writing class. Lou Segusi began volunteering with the campus writing center, and he told me he was considering going on to get a master's degree so he could become an English teacher. He moved in with a friend who had an apartment off-campus for the rest of the term.

Tony Rinaldi got a search warrant for Juan and Jose's room, based on the steroids Rochester found and Mike MacCormac's confession that he had been buying from them. Babson had a long talk with Mike, and Babson said he could keep his job if he submitted to periodic drug tests.

Juan and Jose rolled on the dealer who had been supplying them with the steroids, back in their home town of Jersey City. They were both released on bail, but because they had been selling to fellow students as well as Mike, they were both expelled. I was glad to see them go, and I'm sure Lou was, too. A couple of weeks later, after his cast was off, a pretty, dark-haired girl met him outside the classroom as the tech writing class was finishing. He introduced her as Desiree.

Norah Leedom announced that she was retiring from Eastern at the end of the semester; she was taking the money from the sale of the land she and Joe had owned in Vermont and financing a long trip overseas. She had a book in mind, she said, about Joe and their life together. I asked if it would include the details of the murder and she said, "No, I'll leave that to some mystery writer."

42379304R10115